CW00695197

BONDED

STAR BREED: BOOK TWO

ELIN WYN

CLOCK
WALK
PUBLISHING

ERIS

*T*he *Nyx* was never all that fast.

She wasn't the sturdiest or most reputable model on the market, even when she was first built—and I got her second- or third-hand. Some of the repairs I had to figure out to get her to run to my satisfaction drove me up the wall.

Worse, some of them sent me outside her, into the vacuum of space, to work on the outer hull.

No planet-side mechanics for her—she wasn't the kind of ship that was ever meant to land, and after a decade or so of technological advances, most everyone had left models like her behind.

But what the *Nyx* lacked in brawn or speed, she made up for in brains. She was thorough, and curious, and once I'd gotten my hands on her programming and customized everything to my satisfaction, she even had a winning personality.

In our time together, I'd taught her everything I knew, and, together, the two of us made the best damn salvaging team in the Empire.

Well, at least out here in the fringes.

We'd been moving further out the past several years, since most of the asteroid fields in the center of the Empire were pretty well picked-over. As we'd gone further afield, I'd slowly lost contact with everyone I'd known, our messages getting fewer and farther between.

Nixie didn't care—she was a computer, and she had me all to herself.

As far as I was concerned, it was an additional plus. It was already worth it to be off-planet. On *Nyx,* the gravity was much lighter than on planet-side, and I never had to deal with crowds or uncomfortably distant horizons.

"There is no evidence that the wreck has been boarded since shut-down," Nixie said in my ear as I began the sequence to seal up my suit. *"Despite its size, the wreck is hidden effectively from most scanners, as a blip that verifies at roughly 5%. It is also surrounded by other, more noticeable, false positives, both to my scanners and probably also to the naked human eye."*

"Hmm. Sounds like someone wants to hide something." I double-checked the readouts projected onto the visor of my helmet, getting ready to head out into the biggest, darkest unknown. "How long do you think it's been there?"

Nixie paused before answering. *"Unknown. Judging by the ambient temperature of the craft, it has been at least four weeks since the engines have run at standard capacity. It could be as many as six, however."*

"That's a pretty wide margin of error for you," I said, wary.

Most goods worth salvaging didn't come with an expiration date, but the longer a ship had been down, the bigger the chance whatever it had carried would be damaged—or already gone, picked up by someone else.

If Nixie had a nose, she would have sniffed. *"After a certain threshold, cooling is difficult to model, especially in the presence of unknown variables such as—"*

I chuckled. "Okay, girl, I get it. Maybe a month, maybe two?"

"I may be able to give you a more accurate report once you have completed standard reconnaissance," she said, sounding mollified.

"Point taken." Waiting for the air to be drained from the airlock, I double-checked the line I'd be using to abseil over to the ship. "Anything else you can tell me?"

"*Damage to the ship's hull and power systems indicates that she may have been disabled by offensive fire,*" Nixie said over my headset. Her voice was even more metallic than usual in the tiny speakers.

"Attacked, then."

"*It appears so.*"

I whistled silently; that was kind of a mixed bag.

On the one hand, there was sometimes really good freight on ships that had met more violent ends. On the other, there were often much less pleasant leavings, too—the sort of things I'd have nightmares about later.

"Thanks for the warning," I mumbled. Then, before I could lose my nerve, I added, "Fire."

Nixie obliged. I squinted, trying to see the rappel line as it vanished into the distance, but I couldn't be sure it had hit the ship until Nixie gave me the all-clear.

When she did, I triple-checked, as always, to make sure my carabiner was secure. "Keep comms open unless I tell you to take them down, okay? Same goes for main power. And keep an eye out for strangers—ping me if you pick up anything."

"*Understood.*"

I gave Nixie the same orders any time I was away salvaging, but she was a good sport about it, at least. We hadn't had any excitement in a little while, so she was probably enjoying herself at least as much as I was.

"Here I go," I said, and pushed myself through the airlock doors and out into the blackness.

SPACE IS BIG. You can't really say much more than that about it, because when it comes to the scales involved in astronomy as a whole, only understatement can come anywhere close to getting the point across.

Here's another understatement: I've never liked big places. All the planet-dwellers I'd met tended to complain that space stations are too cramped, but even they were big enough to bother me-- and the number of people in them didn't help.

So, the part of my job when I was stuck floating with only a few inches of plastic and metal to separate my body from literally the biggest thing there was? Not my favorite. I dealt with it, though, because the rest of that job was awesome enough to make up for it.

I tried not to think about anything but the ship in front of me, the line I was firing over to it, and how I was going to get the airlock open. Fortunately, most airlocks came with suit-recognition that operated on battery power; it helped minimize accidents, with the added bonus of making my job easier.

Better still, there was enough power that the airlock worked correctly, letting me in, shutting behind me, and filtering air into the room. I moved to take off my helmet.

"You shouldn't do that," Nixie's voice said in my ear. *"'Never trust a flotsam ship's systems until you've seen its own diagnostics.' You programmed that into me yourself."*

"Oh, fine, I'll leave it on." I liked tight spaces, sure, but ship's corridors weren't built to accommodate vacuum suits.

It wasn't a model I was familiar with, and I was familiar with most ship models at this point, especially the older ones.

There were signs of damage, too, I noticed as I traversed the hallways. Probably a few serious impacts; the lights were down or flickering in some sections of the hallway, and the temperature regulation system was working irregularly. Whatever had hit this ship had barely left it in one piece.

I narrated my findings to Nixie as I went, and she supplemented my reports with things that the sensors in my suit picked up. Together, we compared the internal damage with the external.

It definitely spelled out a fight that whoever was aboard this ship had lost–badly.

The bridge showed enough signs of damage that I was a little reluctant to set foot in it.

Large windows were usually considered a liability in ship-building, but this helm had a window that took up almost an entire wall. There were screens and holographic projection systems everywhere, most of them powered off.

It looked like it was designed to show the ship and its surroundings at every possible angle. The entire setup was more expensive than I'd been expecting, to say the least. It looked a bit like something out of one of the old-fashioned war-drama holos. Except for the lack of bodies. Everyone was long gone.

"Was this thing designed for combat?" I asked Nixie.

"I don't know. I still haven't been able to find a match in my database."

"Hmm." I made my way carefully over to what was probably the captain's chair––it was near the center of the room, and had a large screen attached. "I'll see if there are any logs still in the system."

"If you wanted, I could—"

"No way, girl. You have no idea where this ship's been, you are *not* jacking into it." I unfastened my gloves and searched the side of the screen until I found the wake switch.

Nothing happened.

"All auxiliary power has probably been routed to the life-support systems," Nixie told me.

"Yeah, I was getting there." I stood up and looked around again. There were half a dozen stations around the helm, but the one that I wanted was...

It took me a couple of tries before I figured it out. The screen for the power allocation was the only one to light up right away. "Here we go. Power's being routed to cloaking, even though it's down, so might as well turn that off. Then there's artificial gravity, of course. Life support seems fine…" I trailed off.

"And?" Nixie asked in my ear.

I swallowed. "And suspended animation—two units."

"In use?"

"Seems so." I pulled off my helmet and secured it against the back of my suit, convinced I'd be able to breathe without it. "I guess this ship wasn't quite as abandoned as we thought it was."

I'd never come across live passengers during a salvage before. From what I've heard, it was rare. Passengers on a broken-down ship were usually either rescued immediately, or just plain didn't make it.

And then, of course, most salvagers wouldn't talk much about what they would do if they encountered any. Some of us were more scrupulous than others, and a situation like this started to veer dangerously close to piracy.

Officially, it was my duty to step back now and help any passengers on board. Realistically, not all salvagers did that, and cryo pods were even more of a gray area. Cryogenic pods were expensive, unreliable, and no use if no one ever found them to bring you back.

Most of my peers probably wouldn't judge me too harshly for leaving them as they were and taking everything unessential off the ship. Some probably wouldn't even judge me for switching them off.

Lucky for any possible survivors, it was my call to make rather than someone else's. "Looks like this just turned into a rescue mission," I told Nixie. I double-checked that the power lines to the two pods were secure, made sure I knew how to get there, and then set out.

THE PODS WERE LOCATED in two different parts of the ship. One was in the medbay, and the other was in an unlabeled room nearer to the engines. The medbay was the closer of the two locations, so I decided to start there.

This part of the ship, too, was different than what I'd been expecting. In any normal ship, the medbay would be pretty small and limited to first-aid and stasis only, but this medbay was large and took almost half a deck.

There were half a dozen small chambers set in the walls, some of them locked with security codes, and an entire wall was lined with cryo pods. All were dark except for one, a tiny green light flashing in the corner.

Normally the thing would've had a screen on the front, providing information about the person inside and about how safe the outside environment was for them. This one didn't have anything like that. Instead, there were two buttons, and one of them was already flush with the surface.

There was something embossed at the top of the pod, too—a number and a name. *G01SN0025 - Med2* . That was all—no window to see into the pod, no customization options, no note of any kind to someone who might come along and discover it.

"What are you seeing?" Nixie asked.

"Not enough to know anything more," I said, and then, "I'm just going to open it."

"Are you sure?" When I didn't answer right away, Nixie pressed on. *"Even if you start the interface, it will still probably take between thirty minutes and several hours for the process of reanimation to be—"*

I pushed the button, and the door launched open in a cloud of steam, almost like it had been spring-loaded. It almost hit me in the face.

I flinched back instinctively, but curiosity drew me back. This wasn't how stasis pods were supposed to behave.

I leaned cautiously in towards the pod, trying to get a good look through the dispersing vapor…

And a large, clawed hand wrapped around my throat.

ERIS

I struggled instinctively, but my suit made the movements clumsy; my feet slipped out from under me and I fell partly atop the pod.

My hands scrabbled at its lip as I tried to push myself away. The hand tightened, and I croaked slightly as I was pushed up and away from any support, half-dangling in midair.

The man inside sat up slowly, holding me at arm's length to one side, and we stared at each other.

He had faintly luminous light brown eyes set in a face that was twisted into a snarl under spiky, dark blond hair. His teeth looked almost pointed, and—though it was hard to tell at this angle—his ears looked to be, too.

He gave me a once-over, and then, as I struggled to take a breath, released me suddenly.

I stumbled back until I hit the wall of the medbay and then slid down, one hand rubbing at the skin of my throat. It stung, but I couldn't tell yet if there was any real damage.

When I looked up, he was outside the pod, standing just out of attack range, in a stance like a feral animal waiting to strike.

"Who are you?" he demanded. There was a dangerous edge in his voice that brooked no argument. "What are you doing here?"

"My name's Eris. Eris Vance." I coughed. "I'm a salvager."

"A..." He turned away, swearing under his breath. There was a snarl in his voice that made the hairs on the back of my neck stand up. He rounded on me again. "How long has the ship been down?"

"I don't know!" I said. "Weeks, months - I don't have access to your logs."

He shook his head, taking a few steps to look over the rack of empty pods. "Who else is here? Where's Doc?"

"Yours is the only pod I've touched," I promised. "There's another that had power running to it, looked like in some sort of lab, from the schematics."

Without another word, he turned and left the room at a loping jog. I stared after him blankly.

"*Eris?*" Nixie asked, her voice echoing tinnily out of my helmet. "*What's going on?*"

"One of my rescuees is an ungrateful bastard, is what," I muttered, getting up and rubbing at my throat again. It didn't feel as though it would bruise, but I still couldn't be sure. "The ship is structurally sound, right? He's not going to open a door and suck us out into space?"

"*Correct*," Nixie said. "*Your suit's giving me elevated stress levels, and data that suggests you were just in a series of minor collisions. Perhaps you should leave the ship for now.*"

"Thanks," I told her, "but I started this, and I want to finish it." I did take a moment to put my helmet back on, though, and my gloves, fastening them tightly. See if he could get a grip on me like this, I thought darkly. "I'm going after him."

I stomped out of the medbay and down the hall. The lights were lower here than they'd been on my path to the bridge, and the passages were narrower. I kept bumping into supports and handholds as I moved forward, making stealth impossible.

The stranger might have known where he was going, but I'd have to remember the path from the schematics on the bridge.

What appeared to be storage units lined the hallway, most of them shut tightly and locked. A couple were open, and these were almost entirely empty. A few labeled boxes, the only trace remaining, hinted that they'd been holding crates of ordinary settlers' rations.

At first, I'd thought it was a military ship, but now it looked almost like a colony seeder. What was going on here? To say nothing of the fact that... I wasn't sure what sort of modifications would make someone look like that man had, but I wasn't entirely sure he was...

...Well, I'd worry about that later. For now, I needed to make sure he didn't damage his ship or his fellow crew member, whoever that might be.

The room I was heading for turned out to be some sort of lab, as far as I could tell. Biodegradable coffee cups had never been washed and had instead devolved past the point of mold.

Screens covered the walls, and I could see a couple of really pricey databanks standing under the main desk.

They'd make good salvage, I thought, assuming I could find somewhere to put them.

And assuming this stranger took kindly to someone taking them, which didn't look likely. I put the thought out of my mind for the time being.

Beside the databanks was a second cryo pod, and that was where my survivor was standing. Only...

"What happened here?" the man demanded, turning to me. I caught a glimpse of a body still in the cryo unit over his shoulder. It didn't seem to be moving.

I raised my suited hands, used one to turn on my external speakers. "You know as much as I do," I told him. "More, actually. It looks like the pod was broken."

"When I opened it…" he paused. "It almost looked like it had never been turned on." He shook his head. His nose wrinkled, and I caught a glimpse of teeth. They definitely looked sharper than they should; that hadn't been my imagination. "Never mind," he said softly. "I think she just didn't make it."

"Did you know her, then?" I asked awkwardly.

"Of course." He stood. "She was...important, to me and the rest of the crew. But she's gone now, and so is everyone else."

Damn it. This whole job was going pear-shaped. But, there was only one thing to do. "Do you need a ride anywhere? Or a message sent out?"

"Is there any way you can get this ship in working order again?" he asked finally.

I shook my head. "No, sorry. Your engines were targeted too heavily. It'd need a tow back to a maintenance station, almost an entire rebuild."

"I don't believe that," he stood there, denying reality. I guess I couldn't blame him. Basically, he'd woken up with his entire world gone. It'd make anyone cranky.

"Fine." I headed back the way we'd come. "I'll show you."

WHOEVER THIS GUY WAS—AND whatever he was, because I had my suspicions—he wasn't a bridge officer. I had to explain to him what each of the different screens did and how they all worked together.

He nodded in some places, mainly at the weapons and the navigation stations, but when I started talking about the more technical details, his eyes began to glaze over. "There are automated settings for those sorts of things," he said, waving a hand.

"Yes, but most of them are locked right now because of the power deficit," I explained. "Your ship's bigger than mine, so I couldn't give you much of a power boost, even if it'd help. You could recharge if you weren't outside the range of the nearest solar stream, but I'm not sure the hull could handle the radiation bombardment." I gestured at the faint cracks in the viewing ports. "See?"

He made a face. "Fine, okay, the ship's wrecked, I get it. Why are you showing me this?"

"Because it's your ship," I said. "It won't do anyone any good if you try to fly it off and immediately space yourself."

"Might do you good, though," he said, raising an eyebrow.

"I'm not going to try to sabotage you," I said. "You've already attacked me while I was trying to help; I don't think I'd survive double-crossing you."

He looked away. "That wasn't intentional."

"And *that* wasn't an apology."

He looked away, over at the next screen. "Is this how you figured out where I was?"

He'd found the power schematics. I let the matter drop for now. "Yes," I said.

"And these dark areas—they're the escape pods, right? Were they all jettisoned?"

Had they been? I leaned over to check. The ones in the main bay were gone...and the secondary bay, and also a third row near what appeared to be a rear battle station. How many escape pods had this ship had?

"I think so," I said slowly, indicating each of the sets I'd found. "They're all gone here, and here, and—"

"What about this one?" he interrupted me. A finger jabbed at the screen. The nails on his hand were darker than they should have been, and curved inward slightly; not quite claws, but it was easy to see how I'd made that mistake earlier. I shook my head and forced myself to look where he was pointing.

It was the end of a hallway, not far from the room where we'd found the body. I hadn't even noticed, but there was a single escape pod there. Smaller than the others and hidden in a corner, it was hard to spot even on the schematics.

"That one's still there," I said, surprised.

His hand, still next to mind, balled into an excited, thick-knuckled fist. "Is it operational?"

"I don't know yet," My hands danced over the screen. "Looks like it took some damage during the attack."

"Could it be repaired?"

That made me pause. "Well...maybe. But wouldn't it be easier for me to give you a ride?"

He was silent, and I turned my head to look at him. He was stared down at the schematic, his face only a few inches from mine. I felt something thump unexpectedly in my chest.

"Trust me," he said eventually, still not meeting my eye. "You don't want to get involved in this any more than you already are. Get that thing running, and I'll be out of your hair. You can have anything you want on the ship after I'm done with it. Deal?"

I thought about it, and then, as he turned to look at me, made up my mind. "No deal, because I can't make any promises," I told him. "But I'm willing to give it a try."

THE SHIP'S name was the *Daedalus*. I hadn't bothered looking for a name at first—usually the less I knew about a scavenged ship, the better it was for everyone involved—but now it seemed I might be working with her for a little while. Downed though she might be, it seemed most polite to call her by her name now that we'd be working together.

Nixie was immediately excited when I filled her in about my project, and demanded access to *Daedalus'* systems. I told her she'd have to wait until I'd swept *Daedalus* for bugs or other interference, but promised that when I was done, the databanks were all hers.

The strange man watched me interfacing with Nixie with an odd look on his face. He'd talked before like we'd be working as a team to get the pod fixed up, but there wasn't much he could do until I'd figured out what needed doing in the first place. "You talk to your ship's AI," he said flatly when I paused for breath.

"Yes, I do." I was running down the triage list the emergency system had amassed of the best ways to raise the ceiling on our available power. "What of it?"

"Like it's a person."

"So? She's been a good friend to me over the past few years."

"You're crazy."

"No, you're rude."

"It's not a person."

"Hey, I've got my suspicions about most people, you included," I said lightly…and then froze when I saw him stiffen out of the corner of my eye.

"Um," I continued into the suddenly tense silence.

Then he visibly relaxed, and the moment passed. Had he thought it was a bad joke? "Your ship's named *Nyx*, right? And you named the AI after it?"

"It's what she wanted. She *is* the ship, after all. Essentially." I looked at the list one last time, to be sure of my conclusions, and then grimaced.

"First things first—there's a breach in the hull that's cutting off the backup generators. They won't give us much of a kick out here, but it's better than nothing, and closing the breach will improve the insulation, which should also lower the power expenditure for life support..."

I trailed off, noticing he was staring at me intently. "Too much?" I asked.

"Just a bit. What's it boil down to?"

I made a face. "It boils down to me doing a repair run outside before we get started on the pod," I said. "Tomorrow. It'll take a few hours to get everything together, and I don't know about you, but it's already been a long day for me."

He shrugged and stood. "Do what you want. Comm me if you need anything. I'll be around."

Then he was gone, still without even introducing himself.

I shrugged to myself, checked once again over the ship's schematics, and found my way to the nearest sleeping quarters. The ship wasn't all that uncomfortable, after all, and why bother with all that fuss of the airlock when there were plenty of empty bunks right here?

I turned on my speaker again after making sure I was alone, door sealed behind me.

"Nixie," I said, stripping out of my suit, "You have a complete copy of the Empire's legal code, right?

"*Just plain-text,*" she said. "*I use it to practice my reading comprehension. Why?*"

"See what you can find about animal-human hybrids. I think that guy's been genetically modified, and I want to know what I'm getting into."

It was possible that I was completely wrong about it, but I didn't think so, and, either way, I wanted to be sure.

CONNOR

*W*hat do you do when everything you know is gone, the world has ended, and you slept through it?

I did the only thing I could think of, and headed back to Doc's lab. There was work to be done. First, I sealed her cryo unit. There wouldn't be space to take her when I left in the pod, so this would have to do as her final resting place.

I grinned, despite myself. She'd always said she'd be happy dying in her lab.

She finally had.

But what the hell had happened while I was out?

The room smelt of death, but, beneath it, I could scent the strange woman. My nose wrinkled. Scavenger.

Useful, but no better than a graverobber.

That's not fair, Connor.

Damn it. Even in death, I was going to have Doc looking over my shoulder.

But she was right.

I leaned back in her office chair, looking at the blank screens, mind wheeling through the last hour.

ELIN WYN

Poor woman had come to do a job, expecting an empty ship, and I go and half-strangle her.

The console hummed faintly beneath my hands.

She'd at least gotten some power back to the rest of the systems before locking herself into one of the empty bunks.

Empty. Like the entire ship.

I shook my head, still groggy from the cryo, but there was no time for that. I had to find out what had happened.

At my touch, the keyboard powered up, and I entered my password, hoping the systems weren't too damaged to let me into the bridge logs remotely. Long seconds stretched with no response. Well, then. I closed my eyes, trying to figure what the next steps would be now, until a ghost spoke.

"Connor." I jumped, and instead of the files I'd hoped for, Doc's face filled the screen. Her eyes were bright, but she chewed her lower lip, a sure sign that something wasn't going as she'd planned.

"It should only be you seeing this, but, just in case, you'll forgive me if I'm a little vague."

I stretched a hand out to touch the side of her wrinkled face. The vid shook, and a rack of glassware fell off the shelves. She'd filmed this during the attack. From the angle, she'd sat here, in this room, to record.

"I don't have time for details, but apparently I've been cutting things closer to the wind than I thought. I'm sorry, so sorry. I thought you all were safe."

Another shudder of the frame, harder this time.

"They came during your regeneration, and I couldn't stop the process. I have to believe you'll wake on your own, and find this."

My gut clenched. There was nothing I could have done, but still....

"I've sent your brothers away to wait for orders. I'm afraid they may be waiting a long time."

She looked over her shoulder towards the corridor behind her.

18

Reflexively, I turned, but whatever she'd heard coming for her was long gone.

"I have to go now." She reached towards me, and for a moment I could believe she was still there. "And so do you." Her eyes twinkled, just a bit, until the lights flickered.

"Well, that's my cue. I'd tell you not to hunt for answers, but that'd be silly, wouldn't it?"

She reached for the cam switch, off-screen. "Take care of yourself. All my boys are good. You're one of my favorites, but don't tell the others."

Then darkness.

I sat in the half-light of the glowing blank screen, mind whirling. How had her cryo unit failed? Or had she done something to it deliberately? If she'd sent the Pack away, it would have been for good reason.

All her secrets, her running. She used to joke we'd play both sides of the game and find a third.

And it had all caught up with her.

My claws dug into the arms of the chair.

Whoever had done this, what had they come here for? And did they get it?

And what was I going to do about the curly haired woman who might have just stumbled into a war?

ERIS

$\mathcal{D}$espite being on a ghost ship, I didn't wake until Nixie broke comm silence. *"Good morning, Eris. I found the laws you were looking for."*

I pulled my hair up into a bun tight and neat enough not to get tangled in my helmet later. "Anything interesting?"

"It depends on the nature of his modifications," she told me. *"However, the injection of non-human DNA into human embryos is outlined as illegal in no uncertain terms. Genetic editing is considered acceptable after the age of majority, but only under very strict limitations, and the human immune response makes altering an adult's genes difficult."*

I frowned at myself in the mirror and left, headed for the bridge. "So he was probably modified illegally, is what you're saying."

"With more data on him, I could tell you more." She sounded hopeful. *"The Daedalus' system security check should be complete by now."*

"You really want to get into her databanks, don't you?" I said, amused.

"We have yet to encounter many scientific vessels," Nixie said. *"I believe I will enjoy the supplementary reading material."*

"Yeah, well, try not to learn anything that'll end up classified."

"*I can only promise my utmost discretion.*"

This was why I liked having a full-fledged AI on board. How many captains got to banter with their ship's computers first thing in the morning?

～

THE MAN WAS on the bridge when I got there, leaning back in one of the chairs. He was already watching the door when I came in. Had he heard me coming?

I didn't acknowledge him at first, heading instead for the power allocation interface. It was only after I'd given Nixie access to the system that I turned to look at him, keeping my face carefully neutral.

He didn't seem suspicious, though. Instead, he looked even more worn than he had the night before.

"Morning," I said. "You get any sleep?"

He laughed, the warm, rich sound surprising me. "Not really. You try waking up after a months-long nap. Sleep isn't high on my list."

He pushed to his feet and held out one hand. "Connor Miles. Sorry about yesterday."

The heat of his skin when our hands touched took me aback. "Eris Vance. No worries. Not how I'd want to wake up either."

"Anyway," he continued, dropping his hands back to his sides. "What are we doing today?"

"Emergency repairs on the hull. You can help, if you want, but otherwise you're best off staying out of my way."

"Can't you start on the pod?" Frustration came through in his voice. So much for getting off on a better foot.

"Nope. I need to have a stable environment to work in. I don't know how long repairs are going to take, and I don't want to risk the hull failing on us while I'm eyeballs deep in the pod's engine, do you?"

"Fine," he said, shrugging, but the tension rolled off him. "Got nothing better to do. Where are we headed?"

"Starboard side, anterior hull," I told him. "After I pick up my suit. It won't be very interesting."

He just grunted, shoving his hands into his pockets. He'd changed overnight into a plain crew-neck and cargo pants. Popular choices on ships where the only dress codes were dictated by practicality, but their drab, matching color schemes made them look a bit like military fatigues, the shirt clinging just a bit to his broad chest.

Stop it, Eris, I chided myself. *This is a job. And he's a jerk.* But a hot one, the rest of my body argued.

He followed me across the ship in silence, and I couldn't help but notice that his footfalls were much lighter than my own. I could barely hear him behind me, and, after a while, it started to make me jumpy.

I ended up talking just for an excuse to keep an eye on him. "Were...you able to figure anything out? About what happened, I mean."

"Some," he said. "Enough."

"Oh," I said. "Well, is there anything you'd be willing to—"

"You don't want to know," he said shortly.

"I'd rather be the judge of that," I said.

"If you knew enough to judge, it'd be too late," he rumbled. "Trust me on this."

"Not likely," I muttered. "Can you at least tell me—"

"No."

"—whether there's anything specific I can take off the ship to get a profit out of this?" I persisted, glaring. Hot, yes. Still a jerk.

I'd had my eye on some of the tech already, but I wasn't going to tell him that. "Look, if you want to pretend everything that happened here is classified for some serious reason, that's fine.

But I'm asking you as a professional. You're not going to be able to take this whole ship with you, and I'm guessing you don't want it found. So, what is it safe for me to take?"

He was silent for a long moment, looking straight ahead and ignoring my glances in his direction. "I didn't do much work with inventory," he said eventually. "But I'll check. Don't go snooping around in the ship's records, by the way. They're heavily encrypted, but you might end up with more than you want to find."

"Fine," I said. It wasn't like I personally needed to read them to find out what they contained—if he'd forgotten about Nixie, there was no way I was going to remind him. "Here we are."

It was the last stretch of undamaged hallway before the hull breach. I pulled on my suit the rest of the way, fussing to make sure the gloves were seated perfectly and the suit itself reported no problems.

Then I checked and double-checked the hold of the tether and ran its length under my hands, verifying there were no weak points. As always, I couldn't afford to make any mistakes—when it came to spacewalks, you never could.

"Are you going to be okay?" he asked.

I started to talk, realized he wouldn't be able to hear me, and turned on my speaker. I could barely hear a tinny version of my voice ringing out of the suit.

"I've done this for years," I said. "I'm as safe as anyone's going to be. You'll need to go back to the last hallway. When I open this door, the air's going to rush out. It's only the emergency airlock keeping this corridor habitable."

"Sure." Then he paused. "Will we be able to talk while you're out there?"

"Just go to an intercom panel. Nixie'll patch me through." I waved pointedly at him.

He shrugged and left, still frowning. I ignored him and looked for a secure tether port to attach my spacesuit to. Spaceship hallways always had them at standardized intervals, no matter the model, to aid in repair and rescue should the ship be damaged. I found one and plugged in, checking that both ends were firmly secured. Then I took a deep breath and started the procedure to open the emergency airlock.

I didn't like spacewalks. I never had, and I probably never would, although I had to admit they could pack quite the adrenaline rush.

I wrestled the circular handle on the door around once, twice, three times, and felt the seal start to shift, and the door to start to open.

My tether twitched on the floor of the hallway, beginning to writhe as the air was slowly sucked out. The breeze around me turned quickly into a gale, and, for a moment or two, I had to brace myself against the wall to make sure I wasn't blown out of the airlock. That really wasn't my favorite way to start a spacewalk.

The gale died down to a breeze again, and the airlock doors slid the rest of the way open. I stared into the darkened hallway for a moment or two, and then stepped through the doors into it.

The artificial gravity wasn't completely gone here, which was good, but the damaged systems in the area had weakened it considerably. I launched myself up to the ceiling and switched on the electromagnets on my gloves, landing spider-like beside the first large crack I could see.

Suddenly, loud static crackled in my ear, and I jumped, shrieking a bit. "What the—"

"*It's just me*," came a voice, harsh and too close to my ear. "*Like you said, your AI patched me through.*"

"Right," I said, and took a ragged breath. I checked to make sure I was still firmly attached to the ledge, and forced myself to get my bearings before I could become too nervous. Best to get this over with quickly.

There were multiple breaches in the hull, and the largest

would easily fit me. Through the gaps, I could see faint hints of starlight and stronger light from the nearby sun reflecting on space debris. I took a deep, calming breath, and then, before I could start breathing too quickly, focused on climbing my way up the side of the hull.

"*Is everything alright?*" Connor asked.

"Fine," I said, teeth gritted. I reached the edge of the largest breach and began to feel my way up the side, towards the outer shell of the ship. "I should be outside the outer hull in a minute. I'll start with a bird's-eye view, and then check whether there's anything the systems can tell me."

"*Understood,*" he said, and then, to my surprise, added, "*Be careful.*"

"Always am," I answered automatically, looking over the gap and plotting out my trajectory. I lowered myself into a crouch, turned off the electromagnets on my boots, and pushed off.

I drifted towards the opening a little faster than I'd hoped, and thoughts of ripping open my suit on a jagged edge rushed through my head. I knew the suit was much sturdier than that, but that didn't stop the thoughts from coming.

I shot cleanly through the opening, with only a little bit of scraping at the edges of my suit. The sky opened up over my head, and, as I drifted further away from the ship, it continued to open, until it surrounded me almost completely. The outer hull of the *Daedalus* spread out before me, and I resisted the urge to squeeze my eyes shut tight.

Most of the steps in safe spacewalking were tricky and important, but this was a major one. I waited until I was several dozen meters away from the ship, and then slowly began to clamp on the winch, slowing the cord that was playing out from my suit.

Brake too fast and I would be in danger of going into a spin, or angling myself to crash against the hull. I'd done both before, and neither of them were pleasant. At least stopping slowly gave me the illusion of control.

The meters flashed by, and then crawled, and then stopped. I was hanging in space, relatively immobile.

"...*Eris?*" came the voice in my ear. I flinched in surprise; I'd already almost forgotten Connor was there.

"What?" I snapped.

"*You were muttering to yourself.*"

"Was I?" I hadn't noticed. "Guess I'm not used to company."

Connor was silent for a long moment, and when he spoke again, there was an odd rumble in his voice. "*Are you sure you couldn't use backup? I know how to spacewalk. Sometimes a second pair of eyes can come in handy.*"

"Don't be ridiculous," I snapped. "I am perfectly capable of doing a simple diagnostic on my own. I've—"

"*I'm not saying you can't,*" he snapped back, cutting me off. "*I'm saying you shouldn't have to, if—*"

I was waiting for him to finish, already lining up a cutting reply, when I felt a shudder run through my entire body. At first, I thought it was me—it had to be, what else could it be? But then the cord in front of me started to go slack and I realized this was a much, much bigger problem.

I hadn't seen it because everything was moving relative to me, and I hadn't heard it because I was in my own little bubble of air; but the rumble I heard over the speaker a split-second after confirmed what I was seeing.

The far side of the *Daedalus*—the good side, for the most part—had been struck by debris from the meteoroid field, and the ship had broken free from the mooring it had made against a large asteroid.

We were taking damage and outside the ship wasn't safe. Hell, inside probably wasn't particularly safe either, but it had to be better than out here.

"Nixie, report," I rushed out. "What damage are you reading? How are communications? Is there any debris threatening to get between me and the *Daedalus?*"

"*Crash is still in progress,*" Nixie said. "*Readings made now would be premature. Structural integrity dropping; central command system unaffected.*"

I listened to her reel off reports as I watched the ship settle in front of me. At least none of the debris seemed to be coming my way.

I thought I heard Connor cursing in the background as Nixie spoke, but he must have moved away from the console, because I could only hear him faintly.

When I heard Nixie's voice again, she sounded…different, somehow. Strained, maybe.

"*Power supply failing in the area you left from, Eris. There seem to be some structural integrity issues.*" A pause, and then her next question made the blood freeze in my veins: "*Is your cable secure?*"

I reached down with my gloved fingers, feeling for the cable. I tugged experimentally, only to confirm it was loose and weightless under my hands.

I swore loudly, and optimistically tried to pull myself, hand over hand, back to the ship. I didn't move.

"*What's going on?*" Connor demanded. I ignored him, focusing on pulling as carefully as I could. The hallway was long, and the breach in the hull was ragged. Maybe, just maybe the cord could be tangled in the wreckage, even if it had detached, and I could winch myself in that way.

"*Eris?*"

I shushed him. "Working on it. Nixie, can you see anything?"

"*All external cameras are down in that area,*" Nixie said. "*You're—*"

Something struck my helmet, from behind and without warning, and for a second everything was black.

I spun end over end, fast enough that the stars around me blurred. I blinked stupidly behind my visor, trying to put together what had happened. Struck from behind…a piece of debris, then?

I was in a meteoroid field and Nixie had just said that the side of the ship I was on was basically one big blind spot. She wouldn't have been able to warn me, especially if she was distracted…

I swore again, long and loud, trying to drive away the panic that was suddenly choking me.

"*Eris!*" Connor snapped over the intercom, but even though the speaker was right beside my ear, he sounded distant. Was the *Daedalus'* communication system failing? I was on the wrong damn side for my own ship to be of much help.

I opened my eyes briefly. The scenery outside was still spinning, and I quickly shut them again, taking a deep, calming breath. As I did so, I realized I was feeling lightheaded. The communication system probably wasn't suffering yet, then—it was probably just me.

I coughed once, twice, trying to force the blood back up to my head, and then spoke. "Nixie," I said, and my voice sounded oddly flat in my ears, "do you still have diagnostics on my suit? Is it damaged?"

"*The primary diagnostic system in your suit is down,*" Nixie reported after a moment. "*I believe it may be possible that the oxygen supply has been compromised.*" She paused. "*Please try to remain calm.*"

I bit back a hysterical laugh. "Great." Stars whirled over my head, and for a second I couldn't breathe.

I could, though, and I knew I could. I sucked in one breath, held it a few seconds, and hissed it out again through my teeth.

The *Daedalus* was a gray blur that sped by on each rotation, the *Nyx* a smaller blur that I could only occasionally see out of the corner of my eye.

I focused on the visor inches from my face and the thick layers of vacuum-sealed space suit that were keeping me safe. I pretended I was in a very small ship that was in freefall, not a tiny speck of a human about to be carried off to my certain death.

"*…is? Eris!*"

"I'm here," I gasped. "I'm not hurt. What's going on over there?"

"*Hell if I know,*" he said. "*Your damn ship's computer's talking too fast and I can't make anything out. Look, how long can you last out there?"*

"Several hours," I said. "Maybe. Probably. As long as I don't hyperventilate."

A brief silence, broken by the crackle of static, and then Nixie spoke again, sounding tentative. *"Your air renewal system was damaged in the collision. You should still have at least three-quarters of an hour's worth of air, according to my current calculations, but those may be inaccurate."*

I fought to keep my breaths even. "Wonderful," I said flatly. I was beyond the point of surprise and was a little angry I hadn't seen this newest problem coming. Why had I been naïve enough to ignore the worst-case scenario?

"With that little air, there's no way she could use emergency depressurization to jet back over here," Connor said. *"Is there?"*

"Is that even possible?" That solution wasn't one I'd ever seen in an emergency handbook, but at least it was an idea.

"Normally, yes. Not fabulous, but an option in emergencies," Connor said shortly. "Nyx, *do you have anything that could pick her up? Magnets, clamps?"*

Nixie didn't bother correcting him about her name. *"My outer electromagnets are too strong to be used safely. The clamps, too, are likely to rupture the space suit if used."*

Connor sighed, aggravated. *"Fine. You figure out the nearest airlock to where she is; I'll go get my spacesuit."*

"You can't be serious," I said flatly. "It's too dangerous out here. I just proved that."

"I can handle it." He didn't even sound angry—just determined.

"Have you ever even put on a spacesuit before?"

"Yes," he said shortly, then added, *"The longer I spend talking, the longer it'll take to get you back in here."*

He was right about that, I figured. I thought it over briefly before accepting that I didn't have much of a choice. "...Go."

He went, judging by the radio silence.

"Nixie," I said quietly, "If you have any relaxing ambient noise or anything like that, it would be greatly appreciated."

"*Understood. Searching.*" In the space of a breath, the sound of lapping waves and chimes was ringing through the speakers. I settled back and took a deep breath, pretending I was somewhere where it made sense to hear it.

It was a losing battle, though. I could feel my heart rate picking up slowly but steadily, pounding insistently against my ribs.

Every time I tried to slow down my breathing, my breaths got deeper to compensate, and I still felt like I was drowning. There was nothing out here that was going to calm me down, because a very primal part of me was convinced I was going to die.

Worse, everything logic had to offer said my instincts were making a valid point.

There was a fresh crackle over my loudspeakers. "*This is Connor. Do you read? Am I on the right frequency?*"

"Yes," I said, my voice cracking. I tried again. "Yes, I read you. Where are you?"

"*Are you crying?*" He sounded confused.

"No," I choked out, and realized I was. "Shut up."

"*You didn't strike me as the type.*"

"I'm agoraphobic," I snapped at him. "Space is as big an open space as it gets. Just get me out of here."

"*And so you decided to work on a ship? Good choice.*"

"Ha ha," I said. "Ships are fine. Ships are *great*. And usually spacewalks don't end up like this."

"*Point taken.*" He actually sounded slightly amused. "*Very logical of you. Just hang on for a bit, and I'll do what I can to bring you back.*"

I was suddenly very glad that he was there. Not just because he was going to try to rescue me—though I appreciated that—but because there was someone else who could imagine what I was so afraid of, who could talk to me and keep me calm.

I hadn't had someone to help me out when I was in trouble for a very long time.

If the worst happened and I died out here, Connor at least would know what had happened to me; he might be willing to take Nixie, even—make sure she was as safe and well-looked-after as she could be without me there.

He already carried one person's legacy, if not that of his whole crew, but if I asked him—if it came to that—would he be willing to take another last wish or two?

My musing was interrupted when his voice crackled over the comm again. How long had it been? Five minutes? Twenty? I felt almost like I was half-asleep; maybe my oxygen was already running out. *"I'm opening the airlock now; let me see if I can find you."*

I waited. The stars still spun overhead, much faster than I liked, and far too fast to catch a glimpse of him at this distance. I shut my eyes against my rising nausea; throwing up in my space-suit wouldn't be fun.

"...There you are," he said eventually, and I caught an unexpected note of warmth in his voice. *"Okay, let's do this."*

I gritted my teeth and opened my eyes. The landscape was a harsh mishmash of stark reflected light against the blackness of space. It was still moving too quickly for me to catch a glimpse of him.

"...First launch didn't go far enough," he said after a few minutes, tone brusque. *"Reeling back in now. The second one will go better."*

"You have to switch off the electromagnets at the right time," I told him.

I heard tightly restrained impatience in his voice. *"I'll keep that in mind."*

Maybe a minute later, he spoke again, tone suddenly more urgent. *"Okay, I'm on a good trajectory this time. Keep an eye out for me."*

I forced my eyes open, trying to see past the blur of motion. "I can hardly see the ship," I admitted. "I don't know how I'm supposed to—wait."

One dot, vibrantly white with segments of bright, artificial color, slowly getting bigger on each rotation. "*Yeah, see you, too,*" he grunted. "*Decelerating.*"

He was getting close enough that I could almost tell his velocity. I held my breath as I followed him with my eyes, but felt my throat tighten. He'd almost stopped, but not close enough to reach me. He was only a few yards short, if that, but…

"*This is close enough,*" he said, voice hard. "*Don't make any sudden movements.*"

Obediently, I froze in my suit, still spinning in place. Over the comm, I could hear a strange hissing noise and Connor muttering under his breath.

The hissing cut off and Connor seemed to be drifting closer again. "*Ready?*" he said. "*I'm going to grab you—now!*"

I felt a jerk as his hands locked on my suit at the wrist and shoulder. He pulled me in front of him as we spun wildly together, making a cage with his limbs and locking me against his chest. He braced against his tether line to slow us to a stop, and we hung in silence for a second, just breathing.

"*Feeling any more secure?*" he asked.

I could barely feel his grip through the material of the suit, but it was helping. "Yeah," I gasped. "It's good not to be spinning anymore."

"*Good,*" he said. "*I'll wind us in.*"

He did. The winching wasn't particularly fast, but I could see the ship inching steadily closer to us. I shut my eyes and tried to work through the last of my panic. My heart was hammering, and, even aware of it, I wasn't able to slow it down.

When he spoke again, his voice was soft. "*Are you okay?*"

"Y...yeah," I said. My voice was shakier than I'd thought it would be. "Should have plenty of air to get me back in."

"*I meant in general.*" The rough undertone was still present in his voice. "*What's an agoraphobe doing in deep space by herself? Are you some kind of masochist?*"

"No," I said firmly. "I don't have any problems when I'm in a

33

ship, and I've never had a spacewalk go this wrong before. Besides, it's better than being planet-side."

"If things go wrong planet-side, you usually don't end up dead." He didn't sound amused.

"Usually?" I giggled. The lack of oxygen might have been making things funnier than they were. Maybe.

"Usually," he repeated firmly. Then, *"Hold on tight and get ready to switch your boots on."*

CONNOR

$\mathcal{T}$he slow pull of artificial gravity announced our return to the airlock. The doors sealed behind us as our boots clamped down. At the change in pressure, Eris stumbled, and I pulled her back close to me, my own heart beating too fast at the feel of her body in my arms. Competent, sure. But so fragile. What the hell was she doing here in the Outer Fringe, alone?

The door shut behind us and there was a loud hissing sound as air filtered into the room again.

Then a ding, and her AI informed us the hallway was once again at a standard atmospheric pressure.

Eris squirmed to get free of my grip, to release the gloves' locks and the helmet closure.

I turned away at the sight of the long fall of dark hair that spilled from her helmet, fought to keep my mind on the mission while I stripped off my own gloves. Helmet off, I pushed the suit the rest of the way past my waist.

"Are you alright now?" I asked over my shoulder. She was safe now. Her suit would have to be fixed, but that shouldn't be a problem.

A wave of irrational anger surged through me. Her ability to work in open space despite her terror was impressive, but why was she putting herself through this?

Only silence answered me. I turned back to see her leaning against the wall, eyes closed, face paler than I'd like.

Concern replaced my anger. "What's wrong?" I placed my fingers over her exposed neck to check her pulse. A little fast, but slowing. She nestled her cheek down to rest in my palm, and I froze.

"Just a little lightheaded still" she answered. "I'll get back to a new plan in just a moment."

I bit back a growl of frustration. "You can take more than a moment. Here, let me help you get out of that." I unsealed her suit and began carefully peeling her out of it. As I paused at her hips, unsure how to proceed, she put her hand over mine, stopping me.

Her dark eyes were open now, and she smiled. "You're sweet, as long as you're not woken up suddenly, you know that?"

Her fingers ran back and forth over the back of my hand as she stared for a long moment, before stretching up to place a light kiss on my lips.

I didn't respond. Couldn't, wouldn't respond.

She leaned back against the wall, lines on her forehead.

"Sorry, should have asked first if you were interested." Her eyes widened. "Or single. Oh, Void. For all I know, you had a partner on board, a family." Her cheeks reddened. "I shouldn't have done that. I just thought..." She started to push away, and my hand tightened at her hip.

"No," I pushed out, my voice rough. "No partner."

She tilted her chin up, her color still high. "I shouldn't have assumed that you might be interested."

The smell of her would drive me mad, but still, this couldn't be right. "That's not how you need to thank me, if that's what you thought."

Her eyes flared. "No, I thank you by saying 'thank you.' This," she placed her hand on my chest, ran it up to my shoulder, "is something entirely different."

In a moment of weakness, I dropped my face into the crook of her neck to breathe in her scent. My tongue darted out for just a quick taste before I pulled away. "This isn't a good idea. You don't know what you're getting involved with."

She stepped closer, and my arms wrapped around her as if of their own accord. "Are you going to hurt me?"

"No," my breathing grew heavy, "but you don't even know what I am."

Her hands roamed my back. "I'm not offering marriage, you know," she whispered. "But you did say I should take more than a moment to recover." She nuzzled at my neck. "And I thought, if you were interested, I'd spend those moments with you."

She punctuated her words with tiny nips across my shoulder, each bite winding the tension between us more and more. Until, with her last nip, I snapped.

I lifted her until her lips met mine, plundering her mouth, tasting her sweetness until she gasped for air, clinging to my shoulders.

"I'm interested," I growled.

She kissed me hard, and my hands ranged down her sides, cupping her hips even as her fingers pressed into my back, answering every one of my demands with her own.

Her legs wrapped around my waist, freeing my hands to further explore her luscious body. She was strong, had to be for the sort of work she did, but soft and enticing in all the right ways. My fingers dug into her hips as I pulled her closer, grinding her core against me until she moaned into my mouth.

The sound of her pleasure sparked a wave of lightning through my belly. The urge to strip her, take her hard and fast against the corridor wall, coursed in my blood until all I could hear was her cries against me.

I stopped, gasping, and her lids fluttered open, soft and

confused. "What?" she murmured, swollen lips begging for attention.

"I'm not fucking you against the wall," I muttered, as I cradled her against my chest. "Come on."

Only hard lessons of life in space reminded me to scoop up our helmets before loping towards my quarters. Her tongue danced over my neck and collarbone, and more than once I thought about stopping at the closest berth.

But I wanted her in my bed, her scent mixed with mine alone.

The corridors of the ship had never seemed so endless, until finally I slid open the door to my quarters and lay Eris like a feast before me on the bed.

I ran my hands through the dark cascade of her hair and she quivered beneath me. Burying my face in her neck, I nipped at the shell of her ear, her squirms and gasps like a drug. "Tell me to stop," I breathed. "Soon I won't be able to."

Her nails skimmed down the skin of my back, and I reared up over her, a shout half-forced from my throat.

Her eyes sparkled as she licked her lips, a slow invitation. "Keep going."

I tore my shirt off and fell on her, her words unleashing a desperate need to taste her everywhere, to see her bared entirely before me. Her thin bodysuit taunted me, keeping me away from the scent of her bare skin. Unsealing it was slow torture, as, micron by micron, Eris lay revealed to my every desire.

Torn between her breast and her mouth, I gently rolled one nipple between my fingers as I flicked my tongue over the seam of her lips. She opened to me, tongue twining with mine as my hand roamed lower, stroking the soft skin of her hip as I pushed the bodysuit further down.

Her hand cupped the back of my head, fingers running through the short-cropped hair at the nape of my neck.

A loud clang reverberated through the room, and we froze.

I tucked Eris beneath my chest as she yelled out, "Nixie, what's going on?"

I could hear her heart pounding in her chest, but whether from our 'few moments of rest' or the shock of the sound, I couldn't tell.

"*Another wave of debris seems to be approaching from the ship's blinded side.*" Nixie's cool voice over the comm washed away the heat that had taken us over, a reminder of the danger we still were in.

I kept her pulled against me as the hull shook with each impact. From the sound, nothing serious, but more than enough to break the mood.

As the last metallic boom faded away, Nixie reported back in. "Running diagnostics. No new damage worth reporting, as yet."

Eris let her get back to checking. The hull of the *Daedalus* could still take minor impacts, and as much as I was reluctant to trust a strange AI, Eris seemed confident in her partner's ability.

I watched her, waiting, wondering how long she'd been alone in that ship. Her expressive face told me she'd shifted from passionate lover to calm professional, thoughts running fast as to our options, the next steps to take.

"I need to get back out there," she started, and fury washed over me as fast as the words left her.

"Not happening," I snapped out.

She rolled her eyes. "I need to patch the hull if we're going to be able to get that pod of yours fixed."

"I'll do it." My arms tightened around her, but she pushed away to sit up on the bunk.

"Do you even know what to look for?" She shrugged back into her bodysuit, and I fought the urge to stroke the supple skin of her bare arm before it was covered.

"No, but I'll learn. You can show me, your AI can show me."

"Seriously?" She stood up, shaking her head. "Hull repair isn't really a job for amateurs."

She moved to the door, but didn't count on my speed. "You're not going back out there," I breathed onto the top of her head, my hands running up and down her arms, willing her to soften, to come back to the bunk, to just stay.

Stay where I could protect her.

The thought startled me enough to give her an opening to snatch up her helmet and slide out the door.

"I may not know what you are, Connor, but I do know one thing." She stood in the corridor, eyes blazing.

"No one tells me what to do."

ERIS

"*E*ris, *I don't think you should go back out there.*"

"What?" I choked. The last thing I expected was my partner, my AI, to side with the control freak.

Sexy control freak.

Did he make my bones melt? Sure, even flicking through the repair specs on the pod, just thinking about his touch made my skin shiver.

Was getting out of his bed way, way harder than it should have been?

Unfortunately, yes.

Was he stuffed to the eyeballs with issues that went beyond whatever had been done to his genes?

Yes.

There was no room in my life for someone who thought he could come in and tell me what to do.

"If I wanted that, I'd have stayed home," I muttered, flipping through data screens, searching for any ammunition in the argument with Nixie that had gone on for over an hour now.

Never fight with an AI. They pretty much always win.

"*There's no need to go out. I've reconfigured the* Daedalus' *hull monitoring system. Any changes in structural stability are now moni-tored to the micron."*

It wasn't like I wanted to go out. But the idea of Connor thinking he'd won made me want to kick something.

"Eris, are you done being irrational?"

There are some things AIs do very, very well. Tact isn't really one of them. I flung myself down in the chair of the office I'd taken over and dialed down the tantrum. Nixie had a point, even if she didn't say it aloud. What would happen to her if there was another accident, and I went out just to prove that lunkhead wrong?

"Fine, I'm finished." I swiveled in the chair, trying to burn off my agitation. "Nixie, what do we have on the dead scientist?" I grumbled. "I want to know what sort of person started all this."

"*Dr. Shannon Lyall,*" Nixie recited. "*Scientist. Sixty-one years old at time of death, according to her Imperial record. A research scientist and executive officer on this ship, though the* Daedalus *was never associated with any military.*"

"Who was she affiliated with, then?" A ship this size would have cost a lot of money, and it wasn't built like an ordinary research vessel.

"*The rest of the data regarding the ship's history is suspect,*" Nixie told me. "*It appears the files containing the ship's true history and purpose are encrypted.*"

I glowered at the screen. "Figures," I muttered. "Can you decrypt it? Look for any outgoing transmissions—people don't always bother with those."

Nixie hesitated. "*Are you sure that—*"

"*Yes,*" I snapped. I knew that I was snooping, and that techni-cally snooping on this level could even be considered illegal, but I was done waiting on anyone to give me answers.

All anger aside—or most of it, anyway—I really didn't know what was going on here, and it seemed that he was pretty territorial where Dr. Lyall was concerned. I had my own back to watch out for, and I wasn't going to let him leave me in the dark.

"*I've found a cache of what appear to be invoices, low-level encryption,*" Nixie said after a minute or two. "*The transmission system used wasn't the Imperial standard, but the end result is easy enough to decrypt now that I've found their private key.*"

"Let me see what you've got," I told her.

Nixie turned on one of the monitors lining the wall and sent me a fast-growing list of files. I picked one of the completed ones at random and started skimming.

"You're right," I said. "These are invoices, mostly—lots of jargon, but they aren't really broken down into much detail. A lot of lump sums."

I was no expert, but when I made a bulk sale on some of the outer worlds, I made sure that the order receipts I got from my buyers were itemized, so I knew what they were paying for which piece. It allowed for fewer misunderstandings. This was just odd.

"Is this all of it?" Maybe there was something I was missing out on.

"*All data under the lightest encryption in the system, at least,*" Nixie said. "*I've never seen security like this before.*"

"I guess she really wanted to protect her research," I said, scrolling through pages of charts and lists of dated payments. I stopped when I found something that looked like an actual message.

All going as planned, I read. *Some of the subjects are more responsive to conditioning than others. Once I've isolated the factors that separate them, I'll be able to move into mass production.*

I thought about Connor, about the rows of cryo units I'd seen lining the walls. "She's talking about people?" I murmured. I felt a little ill, and started scrolling back through the records I'd seen already, looking for numbers. There wasn't much to go by, but from the sense of the message, she must have been talking about hundreds, if not more. Mass production. That just didn't sound good.

"Nixie. Are there any signs this wasn't Dr. Lyall's only ship?"

"*Not that I'm aware of,*" Nixie said.

"And what's the maximum capacity of the *Daedalus*?"

"*For conditions deemed 'safe and humane' by Imperial transit standards, approximately two hundred fifty,*" Nixie rattled off. "*Potentially many more, if adjustments were made to oxygen storage and space for movement.*"

Two hundred fifty was a lot of people for a ship. I'd known the *Daedalus* was big, but I could still hardly imagine it. And yet... "And it still isn't enough," I murmured. "You have a full schematic of the ship by now, right?"

"*The designated purposes of some areas are unspecified,*" Nixie said, "*but yes.*"

"No crates stacked to the ceiling anywhere? Other signs of people being kept in cages?"

"*Nothing aside from the cryo units you've already encountered. There are a fair number of those gathered in a few rooms throughout the ship, perhaps seventy in all.*"

"Seventy, huh."

I thought of how silently Connor moved, his strength. Even seventy men like him would be plenty.

"Nixie, I want you to find anything you can about Lyall's research," I said. "You'll probably have to find a way through the highest-level encryption, but try it. I want to know what was happening here."

And then after that, I'd figure out which authorities I wanted to hand it over to. This was getting too big for me, and it was getting there quickly. If this ended up being something dangerous, I wanted it out of my hands as soon as possible.

"*Understood,*" Nixie said, and then she went silent for a long time. I found a chair in the lab, pulled it over to the monitor, and waited.

"*Eris?*" For the first time since I programmed her up, Nixie sounded uncertain. "*I may have made a mistake.*"

"Is it anything that's going to keep me from getting that pod fixed for Connor and sending him on his merry way and out of my hair?"

Just then, the grumpy bastard in question stalked through the door and perched on the desk next to me.

"We need to talk," he started.

"No, actually, we don't. Unless you've decided you don't want that pod fixed after all."

"*Eris.*" Nixie sounded strained. "*You need to listen to this.*"

Connor threw his hands up in the air and leaned back. "Good luck. She's not listening to anyone."

"*Both of you, stop it.*" We blinked at the speaker. "*We have a situation, and I don't have the protocols to know what to do next.*"

"Go on, we'll take care of it." There's not really a handbook for how to soothe a jumpy AI, but usually we did manage to work it out.

"*Sometime shortly after our arrival, a signal began transmitting from the* Daedalus." If Nixie'd been human, I swear I would have heard her gulp. "*I don't know who it's calling. We've been so busy with everything else, and it's on an odd frequency, so I didn't notice until just a few minutes ago. When you were....*" she paused, and I mentally inserted 'ranting', "*thinking, I thought I might as well get some maintenance work in. And there it was.*"

I glanced at Connor. "Could it be your people? Maybe they set a signal for when you woke up, so they'd know to come back and get you?"

Connor's tawny eyes narrowed, considering. "Possible, but Doc would have said something." His head snapped up. "Nixie, what frequency is it on? And can you find exactly when it started?"

She paused, but only for a millisec. "*I think when we first accessed the logs, trying to find out what happened.*"

"Still could be your people," I argued. If she meant when we first started to break their encryption, well, she could tell me later, when Connor wasn't around.

He didn't look convinced. "What's the frequency?"

"*It's skipping a little, but still, I should have noticed it sooner. It's on sub-space channel 1486.*"

A muscle jumped in his jaw. "Are you certain?"

"*Yes.... now that I have the trace-*"

He cut her off. "Nixie, prepare to jump as soon as Eris is back on board."

"Excuse me?!" Bossing me around was one thing, but if he thought he was going to give orders to my ship, this nonsense was going to stop now.

He grabbed my arms, eyes burning. "There's only one entity that uses that frequency. If they're coming, then you're not going to be here."

I pulled away, my own heart pounding in response to his obvious agitation. "Come on. It could be anyone. Why would people not use an entire channel?"

"Because the Hunters don't like it," he muttered. "And everyone else out here knows enough to stay away from them."

"And you think I'm stupid?"

"No, I think you've been lucky, stayed on the side of right and good, I don't know." He pulled at his short hair, eyes wild for a moment, and I stepped towards him, worried at his overreaction. I placed a hand on his chest, and he quieted, placed his own over mine, covering it completely.

His voice softened. "Would you at least believe that I'd try to protect you?" He ran a thumb down the side of my face, grazing my cheek.

Damn the man. Because I know he would.

Connor must have seen agreement in my face because, without another word, he started out the door, "Where's your suit?" he called out over his shoulder.

"In a bunk next corridor over, but-" I halted. "Connor, the pod isn't repaired yet. If I have to go, so do you."

He came back, tugged at my hand then finally swept me into his arms.

"No, I need to stay here and deal with them." His eyes stayed fixed ahead as he loped towards the residential hall. "I'll use the pod to draw them off."

I wiggled out of his arms. "Now you're being stupid. That pod doesn't even have a secure seal, much least jump capabilities."

He looked past me, and I realized what he wasn't saying. "You're going to try to get killed, aren't you?"

"Regardless of anyone's lack of intelligence," Nixie's cool voice interrupted before he could answer, *"I thought you should know that I've picked up the signature of another ship heading through the asteroid field at unusual speeds. It's not responding to any of my hails."*

Connor's eyes were closed, face grim.

I laced my fingers through his, and gave his hand a small squeeze.

"The Hunters are here," I started, "aren't they?"

He nodded.

"So, we need to either fight, or run. We can't fight."

He started to argue, and I put a finger to his lips. "Not well enough, and you know it."

A smirk crossed his features. "Yeah, maybe I do."

"Then we run. And we make it good."

CONNOR

*I*n her own way, Eris was just as terrifying as the Hunters bearing down upon us.

She shouted orders to her AI while pulling on her suit, mind whirling as fast as light.

"Nixie, start downloading everything from this wreck, and wipe as you go."

"Understood."

"You may not want to - " I started.

"We'll argue about when and what to decrypt later, I'm sure." But she smiled as she said it, and finished sealing her suit, grabbing her helmet from the rack.

"But we still need to draw them off," I argued. "The pod's the best way…." I blinked, then shouted for her AI myself. "Nixie, can you launch the *Daedalus* pod from there?"

Eris understood in a flash. "Sure she can. But can she convince the onboard AI to make it look good?"

For a moment, it was the two of us against the world. Maddening as she could be, with Eris, the screaming emptiness I'd felt since waking up on a ghost ship, quieted.

Nixie sniffed. *"It's very stupid. But I'm sure I can give it detailed instructions."*

"Alright," Eris leaned against the bulkhead. "Show us where the new guy is."

Nixie threw an image up on the nearest screen.

"At least they're approaching at an oblique angle to your ship," I drew the lines between the three vessels, calculating paths.

"For the moment," Eris nodded. "Looks like the closest airlock to the *Nyx* is this one, number five."

I tapped it, thinking. "That's going to put us right in the middle of the debris field. Not the safest place."

She shrugged. "According to you, there isn't a safe place right now. But maybe it'll provide some cover, if they're scanning."

"Maybe I should pilot the pod myself, draw it away. Suited up, it should be fine. You could transfer back to the *Nyx* after they follow me, take a safer path." Crappy plan, but I didn't like any of the options right now.

Eris just rolled her eyes at me and snapped the display off. "Nixie can do anything you can do in that pod, no matter how good your reflexes are."

She was right. And now that the Hunters were here, there was no way I was leaving her unprotected.

There was no way to avoid a spacewalk now. Worse, we probably wouldn't make it back to the *Nyx* before our enemies started shooting at us, but we were out of alternatives.

Nixie tried again to hail the unknown ship, but they maintained silence.

"Are you sure..." Eris trailed off.

"Yes," I said curtly. "Let's do this."

We headed back down the passageway towards the airlock. I paused at an intersection. "My suit's down that way. I'll meet you there in three minutes."

Her lips pressed together with worry, but she nodded, then stretched up on her toes to kiss me hard on the lips.

"For luck," she answered my unspoken question, then continued towards the airlock, muttering commands to her AI as she went.

I spun and loped down the passageways, gaining speed with every step. The memories came even faster. For all the missions, all the time away, all the oddness of how'd we'd been raised, trained, made.... The *Daedalus* was the closest thing I knew to a home.

No matter the mission, this was always base. But without Doc, without my brothers, it was nothing but a floating box.

And if we weren't quick, it would be our tomb.

I skidded as I rounded the corner into my quarters, shoved two survival packs into the carry pouch of my suit and geared up as I ran back to airlock five.

"Nixie, can you launch that escape pod we've been working on in about thirty seconds? Make it look like we're trying to be sneaky." Eris asked when I got there.

"*I can do better than that,*" Nixie said smugly. "*Currently, the* Daedalus' *automated bombardment system is running at roughly 75% capacity.*"

"Forgot this ship had that," Eris said blankly.

I snorted. "Get it running."

The other ship could retaliate any second. We had to get out of here. I knew Eris had to be worried about another spacewalk, no matter how much attitude she'd given me about it.

"Hold still," I muttered, then used a spare grappling line to tether us together, then we sealed our helmets.

With a pull of the switch on the wall, the gravity cut off and only the electromagnets on our feet kept us upright.

"*Just launched the pod,*" Nixie added. "*This is as distracted as they're going to get.*"

"*Understood,*" I said, voice crackling slightly over the suits' connection. To Eris, I added, "Get ready."

Without waiting for an answer, I pulled a grappling gun from its place on the wall by the door to the airlock, and aimed it through the meteoroid field at the *Nyx*'s hull.

If I didn't make the shot the first time, we might not have the time for me to rewind the line to make another attempt.

The end faded quickly from sight. I waited, eyeing the gun, until the readout flashed at the same time Nixie spoke. "*Magnet is attached. Come on over.*"

A sudden impact made the ship tremble under our feet. The Hunter ship was returning fire. Time to go. I wrapped an arm around Eris' waist and together we cut the power to our boots.

Damn it, this was a crappy idea. The Hunter ship and the *Daedalus* kept hammering at each other, blasts and fast-moving rubble flying all around. I pulled Eris tighter against me, wanting to get us the hell out of there as quickly as possible, more scared than I'd ever been that a stray fragment would nick her suit.

Time stretched, until finally the *Nyx* came into clear view, and we floated into the open airlock. Nyxie slammed the door behind us as soon as we were close enough to the deck not to break a bone falling.

Eris stripped out of her suit almost as fast, climbing hand over hand to the helm. I stayed right behind her, and Nixie had the engines hot and ready.

Eris took one quick, deep breath, facing down the controls. "Now."

And we were off, rocketing at an inadvisable speed through the meteoroid field. Nixie let Eris swerve through the field mostly unaided; every time she had to step in to avoid an impending collision, it slowed us down. We hit a handful of the smaller meteoroids as we tore away.

"How are we doing?" I asked, terse.

"*They're closing,*" Nixie said. "*They have more firepower than Imperial regulations—*"

Boom.

"*Hit to the hull,*" Nixie said, far too calm. "*Port side, anterior. Hull exterior holding.*"

"We're almost clear!" Eris assured her. "Nixie, prepare for Drunkard's Walk program."

"*Randomizing now.*"

"Sounds like it might be fun," I forced my voice to a drawl, "but are you sure this is the right time?"

Eris was too busy to bother rolling her eyes, but I could tell I'd pay for the crack later. If there was a later.

"Nixie has a list of every Imperial outpost in the sector within warp range at any point. The chances of anyone following us past three random jumps are," she muttered, flicking something on the control panel, "pretty damn low."

"Have you ever used it before?"

This time she did roll her eyes. "Oddly enough, until I came across you and your ship, it'd really been a theoretical exercise."

Not much to answer there.

Two more strikes against the hull of the *Nyx*, and then, finally, we were in warp.

"Can you see them following us?" Eris asked Nixie.

"*If they are, I can't pick them up.*"

I sat in silence for a little while, chewing on that. I didn't like it, but there weren't any other options at the moment. If I was going to find out what happened on the *Daedalus*, first order of operations would be to survive. "Nixie, did you manage to get the systems wiped?"

"*To the best of my ability,*" Nixie said. "*The systems were already failing when I left them. Some data might be left in the damaged stacks, but even if any of it is recoverable, it will take a long time.*"

"Good." I nodded. "Doc wouldn't have wanted her files in their hands." I cocked an eyebrow. "Not entirely sure what she'd think about you two."

Eris stuck out her tongue, then refocused on the control panel. "We'll be out of warp in a few more minutes. Nixie, prepare the next jump. I want to be out and away before they can pick up our ion trail."

There was the characteristic hum, right on the edge of hearing, that said we were getting ready to drop out of warp. It would happen any moment now.

We dropped back into normal space, drifting above a planet that was a bright, dazzling white in the light from its distant suns.

Eris may not have had much experience with this, but she oriented herself in a split second and kicked us into gear, flying towards the planet, waiting for the warp engines to spin up again.

The faint whine built in my eyes, then sputtered and died. I turned to Eris just as Nixie reported. *"Warp stressors compounded the damage from the last shot against our engines. Jump capabilities are disabled."*

"New plan, new plan," Eris muttered.

Sitting in the cockpit, the despair, the weight of helplessness, hung over me, just as hard as when I'd woken up in the medbay and realized the ship had been deserted.

There was nothing I could do to help Eris get us out of this situation.

I stared at the monitors, as if frustration could force an answer.

There, a flicker of electrical energy on the surface. If this was a registered colony, there was a chance of a manned Imperial station. Not my favorite folks, but right now, their cover might be all that saved us.

"Eris, head to these coordinates - sending to your screen," I bumped the readings from my monitor to hers. A small chance, but better than no witnesses.

"A ship just jumped out of warp behind us," Nixie said, sooner than I'd hoped. Eris kicked up our speed again—she was burning through fuel faster than was wise, but they'd traced us, landed right on our tail. There was no *time*—

I felt the impacts a split second before I heard them. One, two, both on the starboard side. The first hit the engine; the second *was* the engine. Just like that, we were dead in the air.

Pain crossed Eris' face, and I reached across to her. A loosened fragment could have struck her, burning wiring could still deliver a shock.

"Are you hurt?" I asked, but she shook her head and just unbuckled her harness, eyes filled with tears.

"We have to go."

She bent over, punched a few more commands into the board, then headed back out of the cockpit.

"Go where?" but I unbuckled to follow her down the narrow passageway.

"Nixie, aim us for the planet," Eris said over her shoulder as we left the helm behind. "Steepest angle you can get without vaporizing on impact."

We raced to the back of the ship and around a corner, then were thrown against the side of the passage as the ship rocked violently. Half a dozen alarms rang at once, but there was no time to worry about it now.

"Escape pod," Eris explained grimly as she led us to a half-hidden chamber on the bottom hull of the ship. "Hurry."

I wrenched the door open faster than she could have, but waited for her to jump inside. She knew her ship, even down to this last desperate maneuver.

I strapped in across from her. It looked like the pod could hold five, but only if they were very friendly. Even for two it was cramped, our knees practically brushing.

"The *Nyx* is on a course for the planet," Eris said, starting up the controls and setting the launch timing to autopilot. "If she can get at least part of the way into the atmosphere before we launch, we could have a chance."

"Let me guess—this pod wasn't equipped for planetfall."

"Not really, no," she admitted. "Neither is the *Nyx*.. The

shielding may hold, but it wasn't designed for it. Not an adjustment I thought to make, unfortunately."

I grunted my understanding, and we watched Nixie's readouts through the tiny monitor as we came closer to the planet. Definitely survivable, even if it looked like it was halfway through an ice age. Not the thickest atmosphere, which might help a little with reentry. The Hunter ship still gained on us.

There was only so much Nixie could do with auxiliary thrusters from this point on. She hadn't been built for optimal aerodynamics. It was on Eris to find a moment to eject the pod in an instant that wouldn't immediately get us killed, dashed against the *Nyx* during reentry.

We felt the moment the engines came off, snapping one after the other and becoming flashing warnings that covered the rest of the readouts from the *Nyx*. They fell away fairly cleanly, at an angle to our descent.

Then the messages from the *Nyx* began to break down, each garbled diagnostic from her failing ship hitting Eris like a blow.

Then all communications went silent, only the housing of the escape pod shaking apart all around us.

It was time to go.

Eris bit her lip and nodded, hitting the launch button with something between a prayer and a curse.

We dropped away from the rest of the ship, caught an updraft, and began to spin.

The pod's instruments began a countdown as we plummeted closer and closer to the surface.

We should have braced ourselves, but, instead, reached for each other's hands as we fell closer and closer to the surface. For the first time since she'd woken me, she looked lost. Her ship, her life as she knew it, was gone now. And there wasn't a thing I could do about it other than...

"Dibs on naming rights to the new planet."

"What?" She sputtered. "I'm pretty sure it already has a name."

"We don't know that. And it might not even be a good name. Xeron 45-6543 or something. Nothing snappy."

She shook her head, laughing. Mission accomplished.

"Tell you what." I offered. "You can name the next one."

She bit her lip, eyes focused on mine rather than the relentless numbers on the altimeter. "Do you think there will be a next one? Or even a tomorrow?" Eris whispered.

"I promise," I told her, then settled back against my seat, pushing my body into it and bracing as best I could. Across from me, I felt Eris do the same.

All we had to do was survive this, and I'd make damn sure she'd have a next planet.

ERIS

I struggled out of the dark, trying to wake.

Something warm encased me, gently swaying like a hammock. Sleep pulled at me, safe and comfortable, until a sudden gust of bitter cold nipped at my right cheek and ear.

"Come on, honey," a low voice murmured. "This isn't a great place for a nap."

With a snap, the last few hours rushed over me, the attack, the crash.... My eyes flew open, mind filled with one thought: "Where's Nixie?"

Everything looked wrong, at an odd angle, until I realized Connor was holding me, standing with his back against a pale gray tree trunk. Limbs heavy with dark blue needles formed a dome around us, sheltering us from whatever lay outside.

Frantic, I wiggled until he let me down and only the threatened smirk on his face kept me from gasping as ankle-deep snow clung to my legs.

"We're going to hope the colony here has a good supply of kaf," he teased, but I couldn't be bothered.

I tapped on my comm link, trying again and again to raise her. "Come on, girl, answer me...." but there was only silence.

"I didn't think she wouldn't survive the crash, her primary processing unit is shielded." I turned to him, eyes wild. "She has to be out there somewhere, doesn't she?"

"Hey, hey..." He looked worried. "You got smacked with a loose bit of gear when we came down. Otherwise you'd know she's alright. She's an AI. We don't have to worry about her surviving in the cold."

He stripped off his shirt, and wrapped it around me. Thin as it was, the extra layer helped with the shivering I hadn't even noticed.

"You got us down here in one piece. Let me figure out the next steps, alright?

Damn it. There really wasn't any other choice. Up in space, in the cockpit, that's where I belonged. Down here, I didn't have the first idea of how to survive. I shivered again, this time nothing to do with the cold. Helpless wasn't on my list of favorite feelings.

Connor pushed aside one of the draping tree limbs and my heart pounded in my ears. The falling snow and thick forest helped, but outside of our little tree dome, there was no escaping the fact we were outside, and unprotected.

Two, three faltering steps towards the opening, and I froze, paralyzed. The panic on my face must have been readable, as Connor's scowl of confusion quickly cleared and he came back to my side.

"Come on, Eris," he squeezed my hand. "For a woman who can face a space- walk, trees should have no terror."

He was right, of course. But knowing my fear was irrational didn't exactly make it less real.

"Alright, let's try this." His large, warm hand covered my eyes. "Close your eyes, and put on your suit."

"What?" I sputtered. "It's back on the *Nyx*."

"Just do it anyway, run through the motions."

Feeling like an idiot, I imagined pulling the suit on over my legs, tugging it past my hips, sealing it to my throat. Even with my eyes closed, his hand never moved from my face.

"Now what?"

"Put on your helmet, and seal it."

"I thought I was the one that got concussed." I shook my head, but did what the crazy man said. "You're going to have to move your hand for me to get a proper lock, you know."

He chuckled, and for a second I missed his touch.

"All sealed up?"

"In my imaginary suit, sure."

"Then open your eyes."

I don't know what I was expecting. Nothing looked different, we were still surrounded by tree limbs and snow. But, there was the ghost of an idea in my head, that maybe there was something between me and all that nothing.

I took a deep breath and nodded. "Weird, but better."

"Good," he looked satisfied. "If all the landscape starts to bug you, switch your focus to your face mask."

And with that ridiculous piece of advice, he headed back out of the shelter of the tree.

I followed, trying to match my steps to where his footprints had already crushed the snow, but his stride was too long. Worrying about that kept me from looking around too much, but I still saw plenty of snow, and trees, and more trees.

"What sort of hell-begotten place is this?" I wondered.

Connor flashed a smile. "Actually, I kind of like it."

"Now I'm sure you were the one who got hit. What's there to like?"

"The air is fresh, not recycled. And there's all sorts of possibilities out there."

"There's snow. And trees." But I couldn't keep from smiling, just a little bit, at his exuberance.

"It'd be better if we were here on purpose, though."

And like that, we both snapped back to reality. This wasn't a vacation, some pleasure trip. The *Nyx* had been shot down, and only if we were very lucky would our attackers believe we'd gone down with her.

"Come on," he turned away. "Let's see if you've got anything useful in the escape pod."

I followed Connor's broad back around a clump of bristly green trees, and suddenly the escape pod came into view. The cracked hull and gaping hatch hit me like a punch in the gut. The last piece of my ship, just as grounded and broken as I felt.

I dashed tears from my cheeks, silently ordered myself to stop crying. I didn't want to be weak. I wasn't weak, damn it. Besides, the moisture on my skin was freezing, invisible space suit or not.

While I pulled myself together, Connor leapt the two meters up to the open hatch, then easily pulled me up after him. The pod sheltered us from the bitter wind, but the acrid scent of smoke and burning wires made me more than ready to leave.

Connor looked around the tiny space. "I couldn't find where you had emergency supplies stashed." He cocked an eyebrow. "So, either you've done a really cunning job of it, or...." he trailed off.

"There's not much, just some rations." I shrugged. "The pod was never meant for landfall, and the air would only have lasted a few days if we'd been in space. No reason to pack for more than that."

He looked around and sighed. "Then we'll just have to get creative."

Apparently creative meant cutting apart the seats to separate the fabric from the padding. "It's not much, but anything is better than the nothing we have now," he commented while stripping off another hunk of fabric.

At the end, he'd wrapped my feet in half the plastic sheeting that had held the water. "I don't think we're going to have much problem staying hydrated, as long as we can melt snow," he added as he tied the whole mess off with ripped out wires.

"Are you sure that's regular snow?" I stared at my feet, wrapped to twice their normal size. With luck, I'd be able to walk like this.

"Yup." He started wrapping his own feet. "If it were condensed methane, we'd have been dead as soon as the hull cracked to the atmosphere."

"I hate planets," I muttered. "They're always coming up with new ways to try to kill you."

"Space really isn't much better," he stood, and handed me a makeshift poncho and hood. I gave him back his shirt, and watched the strong planes of his chest disappear as he shrugged it back on, then covered himself with the second poncho. Maybe I was still feeling the effects of the crash, because this really wasn't the time to be distracted. Whatever it takes, body. Let's just get through this.

Connor looked around the stripped-down pod one more time. "Anything else you want?"

I'd already grabbed a mini tool kit I'd stashed. There wasn't much else, really. I picked up the strap of the sling I'd fashioned to carry the supplies.

"I can get that." Connor reached for it, but I pulled it close.

"I'm not totally helpless, you know," I hissed. Anger at the whole stupid situation flared through me. "Just because the cold bothers me, and I'm not used to being planet-side, doesn't mean I can't pull my own weight."

I turned and jumped out of the hatch carefully, stumbling just a bit as I landed, but thankfully not enough to completely embarrass myself.

Connor landed soft as a cat beside me, expression wary. "I never said you were helpless, just figured it made more sense for me to haul the provisions. If nothing else, the snow is deeper for you, and you're not used to the gravity here yet."

Just because he was right, didn't mean I was going to give in. "I'm fine," I muttered, and stalked away, back towards our tree shelter.

"Eris?" he called, and I could have strangled the laugh out of his voice. "We need to go the other way."

"Why?" I glared at him. "What's so special about the trees and snow over there?"

"Well, that's where the sounds of machinery are coming from." He headed off without waiting for me, and I struggled to follow.

"Machinery, like a town?" It was too much to hope for. I strained to catch any sounds, but the incessant whistle of wind in the trees was all I heard.

"Could be. Or even an unmanned station. Either way, likely to be shelter."

Shelter, machines. People. Maybe they'd have a way I could retrieve Nixie.

I tried the commlink again, eyes fixed on the trail of holes in the snow Connor left as he plowed through the forest as easily as if we were back shipboard.

"Come in, girl. Come on, Nixie, where are you?"

Nothing but silence. Maybe just her comms were offline, and she was fine. But she'd be lonely, stuck without anything to do, any way of getting help. Lost in my thoughts, cold and miserable, I plodded along, then went crashing down into the snow.

"What the hell?" I sputtered, struggling to get back to my feet. A shooting pain lanced my arm. Great. Trying to break my fall, I'd managed to twist my wrist.

Sitting upright in the snow, I could see I'd tripped right over a branch. Worse, mine were the only footprints. I glanced around frantically. Connor was nowhere to be seen.

"Conn-" I broke off my shout. What else lived in this frozen forest? I hadn't seen or heard anything, but I'd seen vids, knew that all sorts of monsters roamed forests planet-side. Maybe that's why there weren't any people here. I dragged the fallen branch towards me and used it to pull myself to my feet.

A flicker of movement to my side, and I spun, waving the

branch before me like a madwoman. Fear dried my throat. "Stay back," I croaked, but nothing was there.

Another flash, to the other side now. But, when I looked, there was nothing to be seen.

A clump of snow fell off a tree branch and I jumped, biting back my scream. I had to get out of here, find Connor. Did something else move, just past the trees?

Enough's enough, Eris, I scolded myself. Time to stop acting like an idiot.

Follow the footprints. That would work. Pretend the branch was a nice, stout bar of iron, and follow my tracks until I found Connor's again.

I backed out of the clearing, eyes fixed on the trees, waiting for any movement. One step, then another. Nothing moved.

Something touched me from behind and I whirled, bringing down the branch on my attacker.

Connor grabbed it before it came close to his head.

My knees sagged with relief, and he scooped me up into his arms.

"I'm guessing you weren't playing some murderous version of hide and seek?" His light tone barely hid the undercurrent of concern.

"There's something else out there," I shivered in his arms, too afraid to care about my pride for the moment. "It's watching us."

"I wouldn't be surprised." Still carrying me, he tramped out of the glade.

"I can walk, you know."

He sped up to a light jog. "You can prove it later, but we'll make better time this way." He glanced down, expression blank. "Unless you'd rather stay out in the snow longer?"

I shuddered, thinking about the whatever-the-hell it was in the trees. I wanted a solid barrier between me and it, as soon as possible. I might have hated being carried, but Connor certainly qualified as something solid.

My head sagged against his chest, and I relaxed a little into his warmth. Wait a minute...

"How are you warm in all of this?" I waved at the unrelenting snow. I took a deep breath. Pissing off the only person who seemed to have an interest in my continued well-being might not be the brightest idea, but I was tired of being in the dark. "What was done to you, up on the ship?"

Connor was silent for a long time, carrying us through the darkening woods. Then, finally, he spoke. "How much do you know already?"

"Nixie started hacking into the *Daedalus'* systems," I admitted— there didn't seem to be much point in hiding it now. "She was just showing them to me when those pirates attacked."

"They weren't pirates, exactly." His jaw tightened. "They were after what Dr. Lyall owed them."

"Which was an army," I said quietly.

His arm tensed around me, ever so slightly. "Yes."

"Was there one, at some point?"

"Yes and no," he said. "There were never enough of us for an army. The doctor never talked about it much, but near the end it became obvious that we were running—that we'd be dead if they found us." He looked grim. "I thought that they'd already found out what had happened to us, or else that they'd lost us and it would stay that way for a little longer. I didn't think they were an immediate threat. I'm sorry."

"It's...not your fault," I said eventually. I wouldn't say it was okay; I couldn't. Not when I was grounded and Nixie lost some- where out there, in the cold, without me. But that didn't mean I blamed him, especially given how much effort he'd put into helping me since then.

"No, I should have mentioned it," he insisted.

There wasn't much use worrying about it now, though. I decided to see if he'd make it up to me with info, instead. "Can you tell me what happened?"

"It's a pretty long story," he said, "but I can give you something to start with, I guess."

He stayed silent after that, apparently waiting for a question to start with. "What was Dr. Lyall doing?" I tried.

He huffed. "Good question. It started out as some kind of genetic research, I think. Then she got her funding cut for unethical research practices, and cut her ties with the Empire."

"Do you know...what she did?" I asked tentatively.

He shrugged. "It's one thing to study cross-breed embryos, but part-human ones were already right on the edge of legal. Then she stole them, and tried to hold onto them until they were viable."

"Did it work?"

"Not the way she wanted. But she smuggled out her research before it could be destroyed by Imperial officials, along with every scrap of funding she could salvage. She went into hiding, and started looking for other ways to continue her research."

"Like what?"

"Unlicensed medical practice, mostly," he said. "She had some patients on the *Daedalus*, once or twice. We were instructed to keep out of sight when they came aboard."

"What sorts of treatments?"

"She never told us," he said. "The rumors were pretty impressive, though."

I could believe it. I shivered. "And... what about you?"

"We were her 'keystone project.'" I could hear the air quotes in his words. "In theory, she was making an army for a rebel faction on the edge worlds. In practice, she was lying to them through her teeth. She didn't care whose money she was using, as long as she could do what she wanted with it."

"She did make you, though, right?" I pointed out.

"Yes, but she promised them an army." He grinned humorlessly. "The *Daedalus* was big, but not that big. There was no way she could have provided that to any decent standard."

I thought about the invoices I'd seen. "So, what did she do?" I asked, almost dreading the answer.

But Connor looked amused. "She told them she was using a whole lot of methods she wasn't," he said. "If you saw any of her invoices...she made most of that up. She'd joke about it sometimes. She made them think that she harvested human and animal remains, and kept us in kennels with brainwashing instead of training. For the amount they were paying, they thought they were getting a miracle."

"So they didn't look at it too closely," I guessed.

"Exactly. She used to say that all revolutionaries are idealists at heart. They didn't really want to know what she was doing to us, and she dropped plenty of hints to keep it that way."

That made enough sense, I supposed. And for a mad scientist, I had to admit that Dr. Lyall was a bit more likable than I'd been expecting. But still...

"Why do it at all?" I asked carefully.

Connor sighed. "I'm not sure. We weren't exactly encouraged to ask questions. But...well." He shrugged. "I guess it was her way of leaving her mark on the universe. Just making these hybrid organisms and setting them loose on the other worlds, like it was her way of proving she existed."

Just because she could? I thought about it, and shivered. "Are the...others like you?"

"Maybe not quite as friendly," he said, and I couldn't tell if he was joking. He looked at me out of the corner of his eye, half-smiling. "That it for your questions?"

Not hardly. But it was more information than I'd had, more than I'd expected him to give me.

"I'll keep for now," I said and tried to refrain from pressing further into his chest, away from the cold.

He noticed my slight movement and looked down, frowning.

"We need to decide between stopping for the night, starting a fire and getting you warmed up, or..."

"Or?"

"I can keep moving through the dark for a while yet, see how much closer we can get to that outpost I heard."

I still didn't hear a damn thing.

"If I wasn't here, what would you do?"

He shrugged. "Keep going, on the off-chance that my objective was that outpost. But, that's an irrational question. You are here and there's little point in us staying alive so far if I'm going to let you freeze to death now."

I nodded, tucking the chilled tips of my fingers under my arms.

"A break might not be a bad idea," I admitted reluctantly. "When I fell the snow got everywhere. More than a few of my layers ended up damp."

The frown turned into scowl. "You should've said something sooner. I'll keep an eye out for the next suitable campsite."

I rolled my eyes at his tone. Seriously, who did he think he was?

Any further mental bitching was cut off when what felt like a ton of bricks slammed into us from the side.

Connor managed somehow to wrap around me and roll, but we still tumbled hard into the snow. Another silent strike hit, and we fell apart.

My back slammed into the trunk of a tree, snow showering all around me in clumps. I pushed up onto my elbows, eyes blinking and chest screaming in pain.

"What the hell was-" I broke off in shock.

A creature of nightmares pinned Connor to the snow. Long white fur covered a lean body and six jointed legs, like an arctic wolf mated to a spider. Sort of.

A long muzzle filled with wicked teeth strained towards his neck while the front two legs pulled him close to the gaping maw.

Connor's hands forced the creature's jaws open, twisting it

away from him. At the side of its head a row of three eyes gleamed a baleful red.

With the help of the trunk, I lurched to my feet, ignoring the stab of pain in my ribs.

A branch on the ground caught my eye. Better than nothing, right?

Roaring loud enough to drown my doubts, I charged the monster and clobbered it as hard as I could.

The branch shattered into rotted bits over the furred back, but the creature froze, then slowly wrenched its unblinking red eyes towards me.

"Eris," Connor shouted. "Get out of here!"

I scrambled back, hands reaching for another branch, a rock, anything.

Nothing.

The front pair of legs picked Connor up, and threw him away. A sharp crack as he landed stabbed me in the gut. Something must be broken. Or worse.

The monster turned towards me, one soundless step in the snow after another.

"Good boy," I muttered as I crab-walked backwards, then bumped against a tree trunk. Nowhere left to run.

My fingers wrapped around another broken branch, but I was rigid, pinned by those eyes. I'd get one chance, and it probably wouldn't amount to much. But I waited until the hot rancid breath nearly choked me.

Then I shoved the broken end of the branch into the row of eyes. It reared back, swiping at me as I cowered against the tree. One claw snagged my poncho at the throat, and it pulled me towards it... but, before I could scream, it was gone.

The crash and squeals of battle filled the clearing as I crept out from beneath the tree's shelter. Across the path, Connor rode the beast like some old vid-star cowboy, his hands wrenching its neck around, until, with a sudden, sickening snap, the creature collapsed beneath him.

I stumbled towards him, my heartbeat pounding in my ears, the copper taste of blood in my mouth.

He pushed away from the carcass and grabbed me before I fell again.

"What the hell did you think you were doing?" he muttered into my hair.

I shuddered, whether from terror or cold, I couldn't tell anymore. "I'm dead out here without you. I know that. And you couldn't fight, not pinned. I was giving us a chance."

His eyes closed, and I caught a look of pain flitting across his face. "And it was smart and brave, and almost gave me a heart attack."

CONNOR

*E*ris gave a shaky grin as she looked up at me. "But not quite yet, right?"

"Not yet." Maybe not, but I didn't want to think about the terror that had struck like a knife when the creature had turned to attack her.

I walked back to find our path. With luck, we'd reach the settlement before night fall. "Over this way. Getting closer now."

Only silence answered, and I turned to see another of the monsters leap from the treeline towards Eris. She dodged, but I could see it wasn't far enough. There was no way I could keep her from being crushed by its landing, nothing to do but run through the snow and hope she could fight it off for just a few seconds until I reached her side.

A stream of light hit it mid-flank, knocking it off course. It fell into the snow, all six legs splayed and twitching, then gathered itself and ran off into the night.

I grabbed Eris and rolled into the trees with her, as far from her original position as I could manage.

Her eyes were wide and shocky. "I didn't know you had a weapon. Why didn't you use it before?"

"I don't," I forced out from a clenched jaw. "Someone else is here. Someone with a high-powered plasma rifle."

There it was. The sound I'd missed while fighting whatever the hell that beast was. The sound of footsteps in the snow.

Someone was coming, but moving more silently than most.

Slowly I pivoted towards the sound, sliding Eris behind me. She stiffened, and I smothered a grin. "Tell me off later. For now, I need to know you're out of the line of fire."

Her hand slid down my back, and, for a moment, her forehead pressed between my shoulder blades in unspoken agreement.

Wait, or be found?

Whoever was out here was better prepared for the dangers of this planet than we were.

I had to take the chance.

"Hello out there," I called. "Thanks for the assist."

They had taken down the creature, not targeted me or Eris. That had to mean something, right?

Out from the trees came a group of people. Covered by furs rather than any of the high tech insulating fabrics I would've expected, their movements seemed strange and jerky until I looked more closely at their feet.

They were wearing snowshoes of an archaic design. Made sense. As remote as this colony was, they were wise to use the resources all around them. And if attacks by creatures like that were common, they'd have plenty of guts to lace the wooden frames.

There were four figures. One continued towards us while three fanned out behind. Their weapons weren't raised, but it wasn't hard to notice that in an instant Eris and I could be pinned.

At the very least, a well-trained hunting party.

The leader stopped in front of us, head tilted slightly to the side as if trying to figure out what to make of us.

Covered head to toe, other than general size and height, I couldn't make anything out. Shorter than me, lighter than me, but still they moved with a certain assurance that let me know this was someone comfortable in their own body.

A flattened hat of brown fur came down in panels brushing the figure's shoulder. A slightly thinner panel covered the face, leaving only dark eyes staring at us through a narrow slit.

Finally, gloved hands pushed the face covering to the side, revealing the sharp features of a woman.

She glanced at the body of the monster, cool gaze taking in the unnatural angle of the neck. "That takes some doing." Her voice was low, sounding rusty and unused.

I nodded a little, wondering where this was going. Seemed an odd time for a casual chat. "Didn't have a whole lot of choice. Hopefully that wasn't anyone's pet."

She laughed. "Yorgs aren't exactly cute even when they're young." She took another long look at us, and I waited, braced for her to say something about my appearance. Instead, she startled us both with a direct, "Who sent you?"

Eris edged out from behind me. "Nobody sent us. Trust me, we're not on this icebox on purpose."

The woman's face went blank for a moment, then she seemed to come to a sudden decision. "Fine. We're going to take a chance you're not from Volsh or one of his competitors." Her eyes raked over both of us, dismissively. "And even Imperial scouts manage to pull off a better landing than that."

Eris slid further around me, and I held her back lightly by sliding an arm around her waist. "They come here on purpose?" she bit out.

I could feel Eris' temper rising and squeezed her lightly. I wasn't thrilled by the newcomer's attitude either, but we needed help. Eris winced, and I refocused.

"Our rough-and-tumble with the whatever-the-hell that is over there didn't do either of us any good. Any chance you got a medic back at your station?"

The woman nodded. "She'll have time to see you." She refastened her face covering and turned away. "Try to keep up."

She and her followers headed through the trees without a single look behind.

I swung Eris back up into my arms, despite her protests.

"I'm perfectly capable of walking, you know." She stopped kicking, though.

"I'm sure, but it doesn't look like those people are in the mood to be out here any longer than needed." Already the gap between us and the group of colonists had grown. If we were here for any length of time, I'd need to get some of those snowshoes myself.

"Do you trust them?" she whispered into my chest.

"Nope." I shifted her, hoping to ease the stab of pain in my back from where the yorg had slammed me into the tree. "But if they've got a medic, and a warm place to stay, we don't have any choice for now." I looked down at her face, lined with worry. "We'll keep an eye out for the fastest way off this … what did you call it? Icebox?"

She grinned, just a bit. "And we'll look for Nixie."

I sighed inwardly. Hunting for the wreck in this forest wouldn't be a joy, but the AI seemed to be the only friend she had. I knew what it was like, too well, to lose everything and everyone in the blink of an eye. "And look for Nixie," I promised.

As the last light faded from the mountain tops, we passed through a heavy gate set into a tall fence. As the gate clanged behind us, the high buzz of electricity filled the air. With those sorts of predators, I didn't blame them for keeping strong defenses.

Within the outer perimeter, the settlement seemed mostly comprised of large and small wooden buildings, creating a strange, rustic feel. If not for the rumble of machinery coming from the middle of town, and the plasma rifles slung over our guides' backs, I could almost believe we'd landed in some pre-tech backwater.

People moved about their business, but, oddly, no one seemed surprised by our presence. We stopped by one of the smaller cabins. Before anyone approached the door, another woman, comparatively lightly bundled, stepped out to greet us.

I looked around for a cam system, alarms, anything, but nothing popped up. Just good timing, I guessed. And, with the last few days we'd had, I'd take it.

"Therra says you tangled with a pair of yorgs," the newcomer said. "You're in better shape than I was expecting." She smiled, and reached out a hand. "I'm Sion, the colony's chief medic. Welcome to Skarth 5."

I put Eris down on the porch, and she wobbled. Before I could reach her, Sion wrapped an arm around Eris' shoulder and guided her inside.

"You'd both better come in," she called over her shoulder. "You look a little unsteady yourself."

I turned to thank our guide, but she'd already left with the rest of her party. Shrugging, I followed the medic and Eris into the cabin.

Warm golden wood panels lined the room, reflecting the fire-light. Eris was already perched at the edge of a platform bed in the corner of the room. Another corner was partitioned off, sanitary facilities, at a guess.

"Not what I expected for a clinic," Eris said, reaching her hands towards the flames.

"Getting out of those wet things will warm you faster," Sion answered, placing a stack of clothing on the bed next to Eris. "Would you rather I stepped outside while you change?" She glanced at me. "Or should he? I'm sorry, I'm not sure of your relationship."

My eyes met Eris' and we both grinned. "Complicated seems fair enough." she finally answered. "But he can stay."

After a thorough examination of Eris, Sion confirmed no significant damage. I asked for a few healing packs on my ribs, but waved off any more detailed exam. Her eyes narrowed a bit, as she noticed the shape of my ears, glanced a little too long at my mouth, wondering. But she didn't ask for any explanations, and I didn't offer. Maybe they had secrets of their own here.

"When Therra reported a yorg attack, I prepared for much worse injuries," Sion commented as she packed medical supplies back into a case.

"I guess we got lucky." A thin blade of worry at the question caressed my spine. We should have come up with a cover story on the hike in. I really didn't want to get into this, not until I'd had a chance to talk with Eris more, figure out our next steps.

Eris snorted, but looked at me steadily. "Not sure if I'd call it lucky, after that malfunction on the ship caused us to bail."

Smart. Until we knew more about the colonists here, I wasn't comfortable telling them about the attack on the *Nyx*. Looked like Eris had read my mind.

Sion looked between us, but said nothing, just began to pull on a coat. "I'll check on you in the morning, then."

"You're leaving us here?" Eris asked, my own confusion written on her face.

"Unless you want me to spend the night with you, yes." Sion looked amused.

I glanced around, lost. "Isn't this your clinic?"

She laughed. "No, of course not. When we heard there was company, Lanko volunteered to move out of his quarters for a few days. Miko and Barv finished adding a nursery last week, but they won't need it for a few more months."

She nodded to a small kitchen nook as she pulled on a hat, heavy flaps hanging over her ears. "He says there's plenty of food. Help yourself."

Eris bit her lower lip. "I'm not sure how we'll be able to pay him back. Or any of you."

Sion pulled on gloves. "Time to worry about that in the morning."

"And we need to get some messages off planet," I pressed on.

"That's going to have to wait until the morning, too."

"And...."

Sion pointedly stared at Eris yawning, cutting me off with a raised eyebrow.

"In the morning," I answered myself.

I went to check the door after she closed it behind her. The lock was a simple mechanical contraption - rustic and heavy. I'd be surprised if any of the forest's inhabitants could break it. Still, I lifted a heavy carved side table and quietly put it in front of the door.

Just in case.

"What are you doing?" Eris frowned, watching me.

"I think she's right, everything should wait until morning." On the way to bed, I took another pass around the room, picking up and replacing small things, but nothing stood out.

Eris stood by the bed, shaking her head. "If I didn't know you were crazy already, I'd wonder."

Half-asleep already, she pulled off all but her inmost layer of clothing and crawled under the pile of blankets.

"What is this?" I touched the top covering of the bed, small shapes of bright color joined with tiny stitches to make a repeating pattern.

"Get in, already." Eris shifted over while I stripped. "Darkness, you're like my own personal heater." She wrapped around my side as I slid under the covers.

"The blanket thing is called a quilt," she murmured against my shoulder. "My great-grandfather used to make them. Makes something useful out of scraps."

Her body softened as she faded towards sleep, molding around mine.

"We need to be careful here," I whispered into her hair. "There's something not right."

She stiffened. "What do you mean?"

"How did the medic know we were coming? How did whoever know to clear out and vacate the cabin?"

"Commlink, what else?" Eris cracked a sleepy eye at me. "You can't be confused about old tech and new at the same time."

"I'd have heard them talking," I insisted. "No one said anything on the way back to the settlement."

Eris patted my cheek and nestled back against my shoulder. "We'd just been knocked around a bit by that yerg, yurt, yorg thing. I know my ears were ringing. Maybe yours were, too." Her breathing drifted into the steady pattern of sleep.

Maybe it was, from the fight, but I doubted it.

In the morning, one way or another, I'd get answers. To whatever was going on here, and then I'd find what happened to my brothers and the *Daedalus*. I shifted my arm around Eris, matched my breathing to hers.

In the morning.

ERIS

"Well, let's not do that again."

Connor had made a brave attempt at the blackened mess on his plate, but he nodded in agreement.

When Sion said there was food in the kitchen, Connor and I had both assumed she meant some sort of mealpaks, or even dehydrated stores.

Instead, we'd spent an hour figuring out what the produce was in the icebox, how to use the mechanical stove, and how exactly to put ingredients together to make a meal.

Planet-side. Not a place I want to spend any more time than needed.

The knock on the door startled us both. I shoved the remains of our meal into the recycler while Connor opened the door to Therra and an older man I recognized vaguely from our trek to the settlement the night before.

Therra skipped right over any pleasantries. "Sion said you needed to get a message off planet?"

"Mostly arrange for a ride, if we can." I answered. And do a little research on who might have attacked us, I thought, but that didn't seem like something I needed to start the conversation with.

"We don't get a lot of traffic, I'm afraid."

"Well, there's always the Lounge."

Captains' Lounge, the very, very unofficial online market for moving cargo and passengers. If you were already passing from one sector to another, and had an empty cargo hold or stasis chambers, it could be an easy way to pick up a few credits.

I'd certainly scored a few extra paydays that way myself.

The only problem was, this far out of the established routes, it could take a while for someone to be passing by.

I leaned back against the table. "Looks like we might need to make ourselves handy for a while. Anything we can help with?"

Therra looked at Connor, shamelessly appreciating his build. "Not many folks can take down a yorg barehanded." She nodded towards the older man. "I'd be happy to partner you with Waldar, run some extra patrols."

"I think I could handle that," Connor answered.

She turned her attention to me. "I didn't get the feeling you were much of a fighter. I guess we could always use more help separating ore. One of the sorting machines is down, so even an untrained set of hands might be useful."

I unclenched my jaw. Hopefully the wait for a passing ship wouldn't be too long, because I didn't think Therra and I were going to be friends.

"I could help separate, or I could see about fixing the machine. Whatever you think would be the most useful."

Therra looked to the older man behind her, who shrugged. She turned back to me. "Then it sounds like you should talk to Hyso."

They stepped out to give us a little privacy as we dressed for the bitter cold.

As I pulled yet another sweater on, Connor sat down on the bed and looked at me questioningly.

"Still worried about them?" I asked.

"We're not going to get any answers in here," he replied. "But that's not what I wanted to check with you about. Are you going to be okay when we go outside?"

I sat next to him and fidgeted with the edge of the quilt.

Now that the light was better, I could see that it truly was little scraps of all sorts of fabric that had been painstakingly sorted by color and then the design had been created. So much time and effort on something that normally I'd just program from a replicator. Who did something like that?

And, I was stalling.

"I was wondering about that, too," I finally answered. "While we were trying to cook, I realized that during the yorg attack, I hadn't even thought about it. Had too many other things keeping me focused."

"I like you focused on not dying." Connor reached over and tugged my hair. "Keep that up, okay?"

I stuck my tongue out him. "I guess I'll just have to keep my mind very busy today."

Hopefully I wouldn't be spending the day with Therra, but her irritating dismissiveness would certainly keep my mind off almost anything else.

We stepped outside, and for the first time I got a good look at the settlement. From the slightly raised porch, I could see a few rows of neat wooden cabins, facing each other across snow-filled streets. No machinery moved between the houses, but I could hear something in the distance.

Two or three rows of cabins over, I spotted the gray curves of a pair of permisteel domes. Probably part of the original settlement - fast shelter from the elements, easy to secure. And, if I was lucky, where the refinery equipment was housed.

When we joined Therra and Waldar, they turned towards the domes without another word.

And I'd been outside too long already. Time to keep my brain busy. "What are you sorting here, anyway?"

"Black cyprtite," came the short answer.

I stopped in my tracks and looked around again. Black cyprtite was a possible new power source for interstellar travel. The random news blips that came across my feed always called it stunningly expensive and rare.

If the mineral came from here, why wasn't the settlement rolling in credits?

"Is this a new colony?" Maybe it had just started up, hadn't earned back its seed fee?

Waldar answered. "No, been here about 20 years. Most of the folks my age came out after a survey ship found labradium. It paid well enough, but since we found the vein of black, we prioritized."

I followed as our small party continued down the street. "Then, why aren't - "

Therra cut me off. "Anyone ever tell you you ask too many questions?"

Only when they have something to hide, I thought. But I stopped asking. Obviously, I wasn't going to be getting any answers here.

One intersection before we reached the domes, the old man stopped. "Here's where we head out."

Connor squeezed my hand and then moved to join Waldar.

"We'll be back by nightfall, missie." He shot a look upwards at Connor, towering over him. "Don't worry. I'll keep your man safe."

I grinned. Maybe not everyone here was a jerk. "I'd appreciate that, he has a tendency to get into trouble."

Other than Nixie, I'd been on my own for most of the last few years. Didn't want company, didn't seek it out. So the pang of loneliness as Connor rounded a corner and passed from sight was a surprise.

"Are you coming?"

I followed Therra through the airlock style doors of the closest dome. Here, rather than protecting the interior from vacuum, the vestibule kept the heat in.

Warmth swept over me, and I realized how chilled I'd gotten even on our short walk.

As I had hoped, this was where the machinery was. It looked like a good portion of the population of the settlement was in the dome today, as well.

Adults and kids stood by long tables, hand-sorting piles of rocks. Another team took the rocks that had passed some sort of inspection and carefully poured them in the hopper of a large metal contraption.

Further into the dome sat an identical machine, but it was silent, obviously offline.

Therra didn't even bother to take off her hat. "Hyso will be somewhere over there. See if you actually can help."

And, with a shrug, she headed back outside.

Whatever. Waldar had seemed nice enough, and Sion certainly wasn't a massive bitch like Therra, so maybe she was the odd one out. I hoped so, as I gave a small wave to the rows of people silently sorting and made my way back to the other machine.

I followed the sounds of muttered swearing to a metal staircase.

At the top stood a fair-haired boy, standing over a rack of tools, looking nervous.

If this was their plan for getting the second refiner up and running, maybe Therra had a reason to be cranky.

"Hi," I called out as I started up the stairs. "Are you Hyso?"

The boy jumped, and stared at me with wide eyes. If possible, he looked more nervous now, his gaze flicking around, as if someone would come to his rescue.

I stopped. Maybe if I didn't approach too fast, he'd calm down.

"I'm Eris. Therra told me to offer you a hand with the repairs."

He frowned, then shook his head.

"Kid, I'm pretty bad at guessing games."

A clatter from under the hopper drew my attention to a pair of boots sticking out from the machinery.

"Kel, didn't you hear me? Pass me that number seven impacter."

The kid scrambled to grab the right tool and passed inside the small hatch.

"Hyso, I presume?" I called out, louder now.

There was silence and then the boots lengthened and turned into legs until, finally, a tall skinny man with thick blond hair emerged from the machinery.

He stared at me for a minute, then shook his head. "You say Therra sent you? What makes her think you can do me any good?"

"Probably because I told her there wasn't a piece of machinery built I can't put back together." Great, another pissy one. And maybe I hadn't exactly said that, but I'd been fixing junk since I could remember on the space station I'd grown up on.

"Really." He didn't sound convinced. "I could use a break. Why don't you get in there and see if you can see what the problem is."

Once I climbed into the opening of the machine, I was glad I'd shrugged out of my heavy layers almost down to my skin. There was enough room for maintenance, but just barely.

I hadn't worked on a refiner, nothing near this sort of set up, but still...Machinery all worked and connected in pretty much the same way, gears and cranks, pulleys and things. Once I started looking, I could see how it should have been running.

"Why isn't this number six broad-tooth gear connected to anything?" I shouted over my shoulder, after I wiggled and twisted further inside.

"That was faster than I expected," came the laconic reply. "Maybe you'll be useful after all."

We spent the rest of the morning going over the rest of the

refiner, looking for problems. Fix one thing, figure out how to machine another part, and then find where else down the chain of mechanisms things had gotten out of whack.

We broke for lunch, stew served in wooden bowls that we lined up for and then broke up to sit at long, planked wooden tables.

I sat with Kel. Over the course of the morning, he seemed to be more relaxed around me and, if he wasn't a brilliant mechanic, at least he knew a machining gauge from a hammer.

"This is pretty good." I took another spoonful of the stew - spicy, with vegetables and another texture I couldn't recognize.

"Yorg," he mumbled around a mouthful. "So much better than stuff from the vats."

My mind blanked. Real meat, from real animals. A real animal that had just tried to eat me. I took another bite. "I can live with that."

"So, why the rush? And if we needed the machine that badly, how did it get into such bad shape?"

Kel rolled his eyes. "Normally we'd be fine. Didn't used to need it, so it was "easier" to just use it for parts. But now-"

Hyso cuffed the boy on the side of the head as he sat across from me. "Things change." He put a plate of rolls between us, and shot Kel a look.

"So, speaking of anything else, is there a telelink I can use? And maybe scanning equipment? Need to try to get a message to the Lounge, see if I can arrange for a pickup. And I'd like to find what's left of my ship."

The words flew out of me, partially to fill the awkward silence, but now that we weren't working on the puzzle of the refiner, my predicament took hold of my brain and wouldn't let go. "Maybe there will be something worth salvaging out of the crash."

Or someone.

I hoped Nixie had made it, that the tiny box that held her core processors had survived the impact, that she had enough power to keep herself from shutdown.

A terrible thought struck me. Would that be worse? To be alone, unable to communicate? Or to slowly lose power, lost and alone in the mountains? Maybe I should be hoping she'd died quickly.

I shook myself out of that line of thought. It wouldn't do any good to worry either way, nothing to be done until I found the wreckage.

Kel was back to looking worried, nervous, but Hyso interrupted whatever he was going to say.

"Sure, but we've had a pretty crazy magnetic storm the last few weeks. Might be a while before we get the data out."

"I'll take what I can get, thanks."

We worked in silence through the afternoon, imaging parts that had been scavenged for the other machine, sending the data over to the fab box in Hyso's shop and waiting impatiently for it to cure.

I argued it made more sense to shut down the working refiner and let us image from that, but, when I brought it up, both Kel and Hyso shook their heads.

"No time, we've got to process everything we can."

But he didn't say why.

By the end of the day, everyone in the dome was exhausted. A small crew would work through the night processing the last of the hand-sorted ore. We had a set of three pieces in the fab box but they would take the longest to cure, a full 10 hours. Nothing to be done until they were finished.

Sion, looking exhausted, headed our way. I waved at her and she smiled wanly. "Ready to go, kiddo?" she asked while ruffling Kel's hair.

He waved at me and followed her towards the exit.

"Now that the kid's packed away, want to come back to my shop and see if you can get anything through the mag storm?"

I looked at Hyso for a minute before answering. He'd been nothing but helpful, was a good mechanic. But there was something about him that made my skin crawl.

But so far, he was the only one in the whole damn settlement that seemed interested in helping me get a message out, getting off this rock, and finding Nixie.

We headed out and I noticed that, while nobody was exactly unfriendly to Hyso, he didn't take part in any of the little clusters of people making plans for the evening. We passed through the first set of doors and, as he opened the second set to the outside, a stab of panic ran through my gut.

Inside, I'd been so focused on working on the refiner, I'd forgotten that we were planet-side. Now there was no getting away from it.

All right, Eris, just pretend it's an airlock.

I'm sure it says something about the wiring in my brain that I would've been more comfortable stepping into the vacuum of space with only my suit around me than I was right then, walking out into the streets of the settlement.

Hyso's shop was filled with random bits of projects. I could see a half-built modulator in one corner, partially buried by what I guessed might be some sort of hover sled.

"Pardon the mess" he said as he stepped through the waist-high racks of metal. "I've been tinkering with a few things."

"Finish anything up? I glanced around.

"Still tinkering. Tele unit is over here," he gestured and then cleared off an area next to it on the table. "We can mod up some scanning equipment, look for anything that's left of your ship. Not sure if I need to add a whole lot to my little collection here," he laughed and wandered off.

Maybe he was an okay guy, after all. Maybe he was just like me, a little uncomfortable around other people, happier in his own space with his machines.

I could understand that.

I flipped through channels on the port. There didn't seem to be any connection. "You think that mag storm is still blocking transmissions off planet?" I asked.

Hyso shrugged. "Happens pretty often around here." He swiveled the port towards him, took the keyboard, and danced his fingers over it for a bit. "Yeah, no good. We can try again later, if you like."

He turned to the contraption on the workbench. "I've been tinkering with a scanner that works more efficiently down here, despite all of our intrinsic difficulties." He shrugged again, something that seemed almost a tic. "But, again, it honestly may not work until the storm passes."

I stared at the wires, wishing I could think of a way to boost the power enough to counteract the storm's frequency, something, anything that would cut through the background noise and let me scan for Nixie.

But a day of working next to Hyso had shown me one thing - chances were good if I had thought about it, Hyso had, as well. He might have been a bit of a jerk, but he was a solid mechanic.

I leaned back and rubbed my eyes as a wave of tiredness rushed through me. "Thanks, but maybe I should call it a night."

"Yeah, we can schedule a message to go out soon as it clears, the system can ping me a notice and I can let you know as soon as I hear. So..." he trailed off looking at me again in that flat expressionless way that made me more than a little uncomfortable.

"You and that guy, you're a thing?"

A thing. That was probably a good way to put it. At some point, Connor and I should have a talk about what exactly we were, what we would be once we got out of this mess, off this planet. But for now, he was my partner in whatever this craziness was.

"Yeah, we are."

He shrugged and turned back to the device. "Like I said. Sometimes things change. Want me to walk you back to the cabin?

I backed away and pulled on my coat. "I'm pretty sure I'll find it. It seemed like a pretty straight shot to the dome."

I headed out into the night, shivering from more than just the cold. That was more than just a little strange, good mechanic or not.

CONNOR

I knew Eris wouldn't believe it was possible, but I was actually enjoying my outing with Waldar. The older man had serious skills, knew how to move surely and silently throughout the snow-filled forest.

The snowshoes took me a moment to get used to, but, in training, we all had to learn how to move in everything from zero g's to nearly twice that. This was awkward, not impossible. After a while, floating across the snow felt as natural as running.

"With the sort of fence that you've got around the settlement, I'm surprised we're doing foot patrols," I asked at the first break. "Not that I'm arguing, I'd rather be out here than trying to help Eris fix whatever she's gone off to work on."

Even on the break, Waldar hadn't removed any of his heavy layers, just moved his face drape to the side to take a drink. He passed me the canteen before answering. "There's been a series of magnetic storms, wreaks havoc on any of our sensors."

I handed him the canteen back, and he tucked it neatly away into a side pouch.

"A few years back, we tried patrolling with the drones, the younger ones thought that would be the better way to do it. Half the time the stupid things froze up, either the weather or with fried navigational circuits."

Waldar stopped, cocked his ear to listen to the wind, then stood to get ready to move on. "It's better this way. Better to know your land, your home."

I thought about his words as we headed back out. The only home I had known was the *Daedelus*. It was gone now, and everything with it, apparently. This wouldn't be a bad sort of place to make a new start, but that wasn't an option for me, not yet, maybe not ever.

First, I had to figure out what had happened on the ship. Next, well, that was a thought for another time.

We stopped mid-day to take lunch in a shallow cave. Tightly sealed boxes showed this was a regular cache for the settlement. Made sense. On a world like this, I'd want more than a few refuges scattered about, too.

Waldar unslung his pack, rummaged inside for a minute. "Got any particular foods you can't eat, son?"

I shook my head, puzzled. "Not that I know of, why?"

"Didn't know if you had to eat meat." He waved to my teeth, then handed me a sealed parcel. "Didn't think to check before we left this morning."

His casual tone took me aback, but if he wasn't going to ask, I wasn't going to volunteer information. The package was surprisingly hot, and I scolded myself.

Just because these people seemed to prefer a rustic lifestyle, didn't mean they didn't have access to technology.

A slice of some sort of egg-based pie, with vegetables and pieces of meat mixed through it, all baked until fairly solid and wrapped in a pastry, smelled good enough to make my mouth water

I took a bite and nearly groaned. Whatever it was, it was the best thing I'd ever eaten.

"When we're done with patrol, I need to get you to show me

how to make this," I mumbled around another bite. "Or anything, really. Eris and I tried cooking this morning. It wasn't pretty."

Waldar was obviously amused as I made short work of the lunch. But he didn't speak either, until he'd finished his own portion, so I didn't feel like I'd been too rude in gobbling it down.

"I'd be happy to teach you, but it's not much, just some basics." He tossed me the canteen. "Neither you nor your wife knows your way around the kitchen at all, then?"

I took a slow sip as I figured how to answer that. We hadn't been here long enough to get any sense of how traditional, or not, the settlement was. But I didn't want to offend our hosts. Better to run with it now, and hope that Eris didn't smother me in my sleep when she found out.

"I'm afraid not. Both used to ship's rations. Quick, easy, and pretty flavorless."

"She doing alright? She looked a little shaky this morning."

Eris' agoraphobia had been nibbling at the edge of my mind all morning. But while she might forgive me for 'marrying' her, I could be certain she'd be less happy about airing her personal business. "She's fine. Just doesn't get on-planet much. It's a little strange, after so much time ship-board."

"Huh." Waldar packed away the wrappers of his food, sealed the bag. "About the opposite from most of us. I'm probably one of the last who remembers the trip out, the blackness of space."

I blinked. "You mean, no one leaves?"

"Nope. We like our lives pretty well here." He slung the pack over his shoulder and headed back out, leaving me to suit up quickly while wondering how likely it was that everyone in the settlement was as content to stay put.

After lunch, we did another circuit around the perimeter of the settlement. The wind had died down, but I caught the sound of a faint chattering through the trees. When I mentioned it, Waldar looked uneasy but couldn't identify the sound I heard.

"I guess my ears are finally failing," he said gruffly. "Once upon a time I had the sharpest hearing of anyone in the camp. Needed them, too."

I hated to let him think age was getting to him, but I wasn't ready to reveal my secrets to a stranger.

We'd almost completed the circuit when, with a wild shrieking noise, a cluster of long white fur-clad arms scooped Waldar into the trees above.

Without a second thought, I swung up into the low branches. Two, now three, trees away I could see Waldar being passed from hand to hand by what looked like, at first glance, short-bodied men in white fur suits. A scuffle broke out, and I got a clearer view of one outlined by sky.

An extra set of arms and a cluster of red eyes made it clear the creatures were close relatives of the ravening yorgs that had attacked us yesterday.

In a fraction of an instant, the creature crouched and sprang back to its pack- mate, the two scuffling as they swung up and over branches, near where the rest of their troop hugged and pulled at Waldar like a doll.

Screw that.

They weren't the only ones who could jump. I pulled myself into the tree above and followed their path, springing from limb to limb, tree to tree, slowly closing the distance between us.

The icy wind cut through the fluttering of my face draping as I leapt, but there wasn't time to care. If these things were related to the yorgs, I didn't have to stretch my imagination to picture their teeth.

The monkey creatures howled and screamed as I drew closer, chittering and gibbering in anger or terror.

I didn't care which, really.

One by one, they peeled off until, finally, only three kept their hold on Waldar's struggling form.

As I approached, their rank stench filled the winter air. I landed in a crouch on the branch directly above the three remaining, then swung down, slamming my legs into the chest of the outermost creature, knocking it off its perch towards the deep snow below.

The two on either side of Waldar shrieked and tugged him in opposite directions, buying me time to rebalance, move closer. The one closest to me turned, screeching fury at me.

For lack of a clever plan, I punched it in the face.

Honestly, I think I'd needed to punch something since I woke up.

The final attacker hissed, wrapped its second pair of arms tighter around Waldar's torso. It may not have been as developed as humans, but clearly there was an intelligence at work.

The lips pulled back in a grotesque approximation of a smile. Decision made.

Howling, it shoved Waldar off the branch and leapt away. If it couldn't have its new toy, or meal, then no one would.

Without an instant to think, I dove after Waldar. My fingers brushed against the edge of his long coat, but I couldn't snag it.

One of the lower branches hooked the strap of the bag that had held our lunches. Only for a moment, but that's all I needed. I grabbed him as I passed and swung as hard as I could to grab another branch, slowing our descent the best I could with one arm.

At the base of the tree, I propped Waldar up and wished for a med kit. Before long, the older man cracked one eye, winced at the bruises, but overall seemed in better shape than I'd expected.

"Pack of chirls. Never seen them this far south before. Something must have disturbed them." He pushed himself to his feet and glared when I reached to steady him. "Thought you said you and your wife didn't spend much time on planets. They got ships big enough for trees up there now?"

I grinned. "That's just her. I like planets just fine, trees and all."

"Never would have guessed."

ERIS

*H*e was late.

I stared at another long pale root, trying to figure out what it was.

No, I was pretending to care what it was, while I tried to convince myself not to panic.

They were supposed to be back by dark. That had been clear.

But the last light had faded over two hours ago, and still no word.

Maybe if I carved a small piece of the root and tasted it, I'd figure out what to do with it?

I hated wasting food. After seeing the extensive hydroponics chambers on the way back from Hyso's shop, every edible bite was a wonder of engineering.

But, apparently without a manual, because I had no idea what to do with any of the supplies. Fine. It wouldn't be in the food storage area if it was poisonous, right?

I grabbed the white root, then shrugged and pulled out two of the small brown ones, and a long skinny slightly green thing. Cut them all into chunks, stick them in a pan, it had to be some sort of food.

Chopping while looking out the window was a good way to lose a finger, so I had to focus.

And just when I thought I might be getting the hang of it, the door swung open, and all my worries fixed my feet to the floor as surely as if I were wearing magboots on the hull.

The blast of cold air rushed through the room with the bundled form crusted with ice. Connor pulled layers off, and I couldn't tell, but he didn't look hurt.

"Sorry we were late, there was a bit of trouble with more of the local wildlife. Nothing to worry about."

"Were you?" All my worries seemed ridiculous now. "I hadn't noticed."

Connor wandered over to the kitchen area, glancing at the mangled vegetables. "What are you making?"

"Hopefully you're not ravenous," I replied. I eyed the vegetables warily, as if they might turn into something edible, or at least understandable. "I don't know if we can eat these raw, but we'll figure it out."

Connor pulled me into his chest and rested his chin on the top of my head.

"Well, it's not like I married you for your cooking."

"What?" I reared back to stare at him in shock. "Did you hit your head in your little run-in with the charming creatures of this planet?"

"Just a little conversational aside with Waldar. Wanted to give you a heads up." Connor reached around me to sneak a bite of the chopped root, then scrunched up his nose.

"Why would you be talking about our marital status, or lack thereof?" Then I thought about the awkward moment with Hyso in his shop. Not going there. I wiggled my fingers into Connor's side. "Move over or we'll be eating them raw, no matter how many faces you pull."

He jumped and grabbed my wrist, eyes narrowed. "Stop that!"

My mind whirled. "Don't tell me you're ticklish. Big, strong fighter, destroyer of yorgs... and ticklish?"

"It's a minor design flaw!" He backed away from my flexing fingers as I slowly paced towards him.

"Come back here, show me how minor!" I chased him around the small cabin, both of us giggling like loons.

At last I dashed towards him and he grabbed me, lightly tossing me onto the bed in the corner. I rolled, but he caught me, his large hands easily pinning my wrists above my head, body stretched over mine.

Wiggling did nothing to get me free. Connor's eyes darkened. "Do that again," he growled, grinding his pelvis into mine.

Warm pleasure bloomed in my core, and I strained against him, this time wanting nothing more than the feel of his skin against my own.

One hand released my wrists, skimming down my side to work up the loose sweater. His nails brushed my breasts and I arched off the bed.

"Shh," he whispered into my hair. "No asteroid field, no one's shooting at us." Connor nipped the outside of my ear, then worked his way down my neck with a maddening delicacy that melted me, left me groaning at his touch. "For once, we have all night."

The sharp knock at the door caught us both off guard.

Connor rolled off me, landing silently on the floor. I slid off the bed and moved to the kitchen. When my fingers wrapped around the handle of the knife, his eyebrows rose, but he nodded.

But his posture relaxed when he approached the door. Flinging it open, three figures came in - Waldar, Therra and Sion.

Waldar looked over at where I'd been chopping vegetables and shook his head. "Void, boy. You were right. You both need lessons. You weren't even going to peel them, were you?"

He moved into the kitchen space, with a smile that didn't quite reach his eyes. "You go sit and listen, and I'll take care of this. Plenty of time to teach you knife skills later."

I shrugged. "Happy to let someone who knows what they're doing take a whack at it."

I looked at the irregularly sized pieces of roots. Maybe whack wasn't the right word. Give me a wrench any day.

Therra started right in as the four of us sat around the polished wooden table. "My plan had been to lock you up until after everything was over and apologize later."

Sion just shook her head and covered her eyes.

From the kitchen area, Waldar didn't look up from chopping vegetables. "It won't work, girl."

Therra sighed. "And I trust my dad's judgment. So, we're here to ask. Don't get involved in what's coming."

Connor and I looked at each other, but there didn't seem much to say, so we just waited.

Therra resumed the story, looking over our heads. "In about fifteen hours, a ship is coming. Not our regular Imperial visitors." Her hands made fists on the table.

The sound of sizzling broke the silence after her words. With an effort, she continued. "And we're going to give them our ore, every bit of this year's findings, and hope like hell we produce enough to make up our numbers for our next regular visit."

Waldar brought over plates. The hot, colorful vegetables over a pile of some sort of grain smelled amazing. My stomach rumbled, and he cracked a wry smile. "Eat and we'll explain."

Sion took up the thread. "You might have wondered why we weren't so certain about having newcomers here. A month ago, we had another visitor, said his ship crashed in the mountains."

"He lied," Therra cut in, "and we didn't realize it."

I wondered why she seemed as bitter about the lying as anything else, but kept eating the delicious food.

"You see why we're not very trusting right now," Waldar added.

"He stayed with us for two days, said he was sending messages out for a pickup, everything you'd expect," Sion said. "And then took poor little Aggie hostage, the bastard."

"She's six, our headman's only daughter. He and his wife have gone a bit mad over it and I don't blame them." Waldar glanced at Therra.

Even though she seemed more than capable of taking care of herself, I could tell this was a father who wouldn't take a threat to his family lightly.

"Volsh, our guest, had a shuttle pick him and Aggie up from the middle of town, next to the original domes. Said if we want her back, we had to turn over our tithe to him. Gave us a month to finish processing."

I frowned. "Can't you report the attack to the Imperial patrol? Surely, even if they didn't care about the girl, they'd want to keep that much cyprtite from getting on the market. Or worse, having a gang of outlaws experimenting with it."

Therra rolled her eyes. "Yes, we did think about that." Whatever else she was going to say was cut off by a yelp. It looked as if Sion might've kicked her under the table. "The first wave of the magnetic storm came up that night. We sent messages out, but we don't know if anything was received."

"We still don't even know how Volsh and his crew even found us, or knew about the ore," Waldar grumbled. "The refinery and mining areas are usually off limits to visitors. Because of the rarity of cyprtite, all Imperial records have us listed as a resource colony for wood and water. Doesn't exactly put us high on anyone's tourism list."

Therra leaned back in her chair. "We can figure it out later. Either way, we've got to get Aggie back."

Connor put down his utensils neatly by his empty plate and stared into our visitors' eyes, one by one. "None of you are dumb. Why do you think she's alive?"

The room chilled, as if the outside air had come in and crept around the dinner table while we ate.

Sion bit her lips, looked away and then back. "She sent a message before they jumped."

I sat back, thinking about how much or how little time little Aggie would've had to figure out their systems. She'd been under watch, and I hadn't seen much in advanced comms around the settlement for a six-year-old to practice on. Still, they seemed certain, and it was too odd of a point to argue about. "Smart kid," was all I said.

Waldar looked awkward, but Therra cut in, voice flat, brooking no discussion. "She is."

Sion continued. "She said she was scared, that the shuttle docked inside a larger ship. There were five men on board that she could see..." Fury crossed her face, plain to read. "Then the message cut off."

I didn't spend much time around kids. Void, I didn't spend much time around people. But even I could tell this settlement was more like a family than just strangers living in a town. No wonder everyone I'd met acted like they'd had the heart ripped out of them.

I reached over to pat Sion's hand. "We'll do whatever we can do help, I promise."

She smiled. "Aggie's mother is my sister. It's been hard, watching her. It's like she just stopped, frozen solid, when they took Aggie."

Therra pushed away from the table. "We appreciate your help with patrols and with getting the refiner running. Once Volsh and his gang take the ore, we'll be busting hump to get the Imperial tithe ready." She looked grim. "But we don't want any trouble. We just want to get Aggie back and go on about our business."

Surprise ran through me like ice water. I looked at Connor, saw the same bleak knowledge in his eyes. Damn it. I sighed, tightened my grip on Sion's wrist. "You know that's never going to happen."

"What?" Sion's fear reflected in Therra's anger. Therra pushed herself half up from the table, her voice flat, her posture ready for a fight, while Sion seemed as paralyzed as she'd said her sister was.

But they needed to know, they *had* to know. "Gangs like that, they're never going to stop. They'll bleed you dry. It probably won't be long before they land here, take more hostages - kids, anyone."

Connor clarified what I was thinking. "Why wouldn't they take the whole settlement hostage? Then where would you be?"

"Slaves, not hostages," Waldar muttered.

"We're not risking Aggie." Therra pulled on her coat, strode to the door. "Either promise me that you'll let us handle this, or I swear I'll lock you in now.'

Waldar looked apologetic, but it was easy to see he'd back his daughter up.

I turned to the one I thought would be reasonable. "Sion, it's your niece now. What if next time they take the other children? What if they take Kel to keep her company?"

She shook her head, face pale as the snow outside, but stood with Therra and Waldar. "We have to play it their way, their rules."

"They don't have rules," I pleaded.

Connor stood behind me, hands on my shoulders, as if he knew I wanted to leap across the room, shake sense into them. "It's their children. Their choice."

"It's the wrong one," I whispered as they filed out into the night.

"I know," he answered, and all the ways this could go wrong, likely *would* go wrong, hung between us for the rest of the night.

CONNOR

*T*he next morning dawned bright and clear, but just as cold.

Shadows filled Eris' dark eyes. She had slept fitfully through the night, quieting only when I wrapped my arms around her.

"There's nothing we can do about the bandits." I tucked a loose strand of hair back into the long braid she'd thrown over her shoulder. "The settlement has made their own decision."

"I know," she sighed. "I don't even know what we could do. But these seem like good people. I hate that this is happening to them."

"You can at least help with the other half of their problem," I commented as I shrugged on my jacket. "Get that other refiner running. If they can make the tithe before the Imperials arrive, maybe they'll have more weight when they ask for protection against another raid."

She thought about it, evaluated like she seemed to do everything, and then nodded. "At least it's something."

Outside of the cabin, everyone moved in a hurried hush. I helped Waldar and a group of men load the refined ore into rows of gray boxes.

Waldar looked apologetic until I pulled him aside when we

temporarily ran out of boxes to pack. "You know I'm not going to do anything to risk getting the girl back, don't you?"

He leaned back against the side of the building. I wondered how many of the lines marking his face were from his years of working outside in the elements, doing what he loved, and how many were from the stress and fear of the last month.

"I know, lad. But my girl can be pretty heavy handed. I know that, too. And she doesn't take well to being scared."

"No one does," I chuckled bitterly.

"And your wife? You don't think she'll try anything?"

"She's not happy, but she won't get involved. And, about that…"

Another pair of men arrived with a loader of a fresh stack of boxes for us to fill.

Waldar pushed himself up off the wall and patted my shoulder. "Tell me later. Back to work for us."

I almost wished there had been more for us to do. We were ready well before the appointed time, and the tension in the street just wound tighter.

You could smell it in the air.

Eris found me in the crowd and tucked her mittened hand into mine. "We should just go back to the cabin." What sounded like anger in her voice was tinged with sorrow.

"I think we should wait and see what happens. If nothing else, they might need witnesses."

She snorted. "Do you really think we'd show up well in Imperial court?"

It wasn't long before we heard the high-pitched whine of a shuttle breaking atmosphere.

Everyone's attention was on the hot white line above us; it was easy to tuck ourselves on the porch of a cabin I'd spotted earlier on the outskirts of the square. Angled just right, we'd have a view, without being too noticeable.

A squat, gray shuttle circled the settlement twice, then came to a halting landing at the edge of the square. It was an ugly thing, built for no more than four, and only if they were friendly.

The oppressive silence of the crowd held until the rear of the shuttle pivoted down, making a ramp into the melting snow below.

A short, burly man with a dark buzz cut and a thin scar winding down on the left side of his face swaggered down the ramp.

"Petro, you bastard! Why the hell did you keep us waiting? We've been signaling, messaging for the all clear for the last hour. Thought you wanted your girl back."

Waldar had pointed out the headman earlier, when we were loading boxes. He'd been rushing from one sector to the next, too worked up to do anyone any good, just splashing his nerves on everyone else. Which was probably harsh. I couldn't say how I'd act if someone threatened my child, took her from me.

Doc's ghostly voice laughed in my head. *Sure you do, Connor. You'd demolish everything in your way to get her back. But that's not always an option. Not for everyone.*

I grimaced. I missed the old lady, but, damn, she had no room for fools or self-delusion.

Petro stepped from the crowd, towards the shuttle. Maybe it was just the shock of losing his child, getting caught up in all this madness, but I couldn't see leadership in his thin face or curved shoulders. He looked weak, lacking resolve.

I kicked myself. These were civilians. It wasn't their fault they'd gotten caught up in all this.

But if they didn't handle it, Eris and I would be dragged into their chaos.

"We didn't receive any messages, Volsh. Your instruments should've shown that we've been caught in a mag storm - comms have been down pretty much the entire time."

The bandit turned around, his flat gray eyes scanning the crowd, then turned and spit.

"Didn't see any Imperials on the visual scan. And I think you're too chicken to try anything."

"Where is Aggie? Where is my daughter?" Petro's voice broke on the last word.

Volsh twisted his face into a sour grin. "Come on out, kid."

Like a shadow, a small dark-haired girl crept out from the interior of the shuttle. Her eyes were wide, with gray smudges under them, and her thin shirt and pants could've done nothing to protect her from the cold.

She looked around, but she focused on nothing, no one.

"Aggie, sweetheart," Petro called her. She didn't respond.

Something was wrong. Lots of things were wrong, really. But here, something was strangely off. I closed my eyes, scented the air. Maybe the girl was drugged or just too traumatized to feel anything. But the sharp stink of terror, even the blend of fear and longing I would've expected from a hostage, was absent from the air.

"Get back inside, kid," Volsh growled.

She turned to go, and the headman darted forward to grab at her. "No, you can't take her back."

Fast as a shockwave, Volsh's hand snapped forward, striking Petro into the snow.

That might've been reflex.

The smooth drawing of the phaser from his hip, the precise blast of plasma through Petro's skull, was quite deliberate.

From the crowd, a woman's moan grew into a wail, cutting through the air.

"Meet us at the clearing to the east with the goods. One hour." Volsh turned back to go inside the ship without a glance at the crumpled form lying in the snow. "Otherwise, the girl is next."

The frozen spell that had fallen over the crowd broke as the shuttle lifted, gained altitude, and screamed away into the sky.

A woman, her long pale braids spilling out from her hat, rushed to Petro's body.

I closed my eyes, leaned back against the side of the cabin.

Eris took my hand. "There's nothing we could've done. They told us not to get involved. And, even if we had, do you really think Volsh wouldn't have taken that shot?"

Without speaking, I wrapped my arm around her shoulders and pulled her towards me. One moment of peace before the chaos broke. Because it always did.

She nestled her head into my shoulder and an awful thought struck me.

"Even though you didn't know him, are you okay? I can't imagine you wind up seeing a lot of gunplay in your line of work."

She shook her head and her arms tightened around me slightly. "Usually by the time I'm there, everything is done and over, or everyone's cleared out. I've heard stories, I know what the gangs and syndicates are like." She shuddered, just a bit. "But I've never had to come up against them."

"And if I've got anything to do with it, we'll keep it that way."

The rising sound of shouting drew my attention away. Apparently, every member of the settlement had an opinion, and felt like now was the time to express it at the top of their lungs.

I started to roll to the balls of my feet, flex my knees just a bit, just in case.

But the fight wasn't headed our way.

"Enough!" shouted Waldar. "Nobody's happy. I know that. We all know that. But we don't have time for emotion." He looked older than he had just an hour ago. "Right now, we have two choices. Comply, or don't. It's that simple."

A wave of sound broke again then, the blonde woman pushed to her feet and stepped away from the body of her dead husband. She looked around the crowd and everyone dropped their eyes, ashamed for something they'd had no part in, couldn't have done anything about.

Maybe they were just ashamed to be alive when Petro lay dead in the snow.

The blonde woman walked towards us and I tensed, shifting Eris to my side.

"What about you, the two of you haven't said anything." Her voice was low, husky, but if her eyes were reddened with tears, the steel in them was still clear.

"We didn't think you wanted us involved."

The woman laughed. "It's clear none of us have any experience that will do us a damn bit of good right now. We thought we could deal with them. We were wrong."

Eris shot me a look, and I nodded. We hadn't spoken about it but I knew we were in agreement.

She stepped towards the woman, towards the crowd that had drifted our way. Therra stood at one side, Waldar beside her, watching.

"If you fight," Eris said, "you risk the girl's life. But you also risk winning."

I stepped to stand behind her. "If you don't fight, you risk they'll still kill the girl, and whoever else they target next."

A low murmur started through the crowd but stopped suddenly, as if cut by a knife, when the woman sliced her hand to the side.

She closed her eyes, took a deep breath. "If she's not dead, or worse, by now, she will be. I know that. We all do."

She opened her eyes, the bright blue drilling into mine. "Waldar says you move like nothing he's ever seen. It's a lot to ask, but I'll ask it anyway."

She paused, and I almost flinched from the pain and fury unmasked on her face.

"Kill them all."

ERIS

*T*he deadline clicked off in everyone's heads, as inescapable as if a giant chrono hung above the settlement, counting off the seconds.

Connor turned to me. "I've got an idea that might work. But I need to know if you can jam a ship's navigation remotely, keep it grounded once it's down."

I blinked, mind spinning. "Sure, I think. If I had my tools, but I don't." I thought of items I'd seen in Hyso's workshop. "There was a magnetic converter in Hyso's shop. And an old flux capacitor. If somewhere he also has a radio displacer, it might work."

"Can you get it done in fifty minutes?"

The beginnings of blueprints, of wiring structures hovered in my vision. "I think so, maybe." I swallowed down the fear. "I can do it."

Connor pulled me to him, his lips scorching on mine. "I trust you."

Kel ran up to us. "I'll help," he chirped.

Therra strode over, dragging Hyso behind her. "Take Hyso. He's the best mechanic we've got. Anything you need from his shop, use."

Hyso cut in. "Wait a minute. Some of that stuff-"

Therra shot him a look that should have frozen the blood in his veins. "If you think it's necessary," her voice dripped ice colder than the frigid wastes surrounding the camp, "keep a log of what she uses."

"Void," Hyso muttered as he headed off to his shop, "I was just saying."

I rolled my eyes and turned back to Connor. "Whatever you do, stay safe."

He grinned." We weren't exactly built for safe." He dropped another kiss on my forehead. "What we were built for is this."

As I walked away, I heard Connor, Therra, and Waldar shouting to the crowd, sorting people into groups based on their fighting or hunting capabilities.

Whatever his plan was, I'd have to trust him to be able to do it and come out on the other side. Come home to me.

I didn't know when that had become so important, but it had. I might not know why he needed me to build something to keep the ship grounded, but, dammit, I could do that.

Hyso threw open the shop doors and I gazed with only slight amounts of despair at the racks of junk strewn across the work-benches.

Even if he was a grumpy bastard, Hyso knew what he was doing. There wasn't enough time to worry about what Connor was doing to get ready for the ship's arrival. The three of us grabbed parts and wired and soldered in a wild frenzy.

Kel was as good as his word. I had only to start to ask for a tool or a part and he found it. Once he figured out what I was doing, he cleared a second workbench and brought over any parts he thought might be helpful, just in case.

Anything that could project a magnetic field, anything that would amplify it. Anything that could be pushed past its design specs to serve.

Hyso shook his head over the soldering gun. "I don't know if this is going to work, but I gotta say it's pretty brilliant." He grinned. "Feel free to rummage around in my parts anytime."

His eyebrows waggled and I shoved down my repulsion. Maybe he was just one of those guys who didn't know when to stop, but right now, I needed his skills.

Right now, Connor needed every mech I could find.

I checked the chrono, calculated the time left against what was left on the checklist in my brain and pressed to move faster.

"Kel, hand me that-"

"Here you go."

At least one of the men in the workshop wasn't a creep. I took the spindrill and kept working, the seconds flying by.

CONNOR

$\mathcal{I}$ looked over the group of people Therra and Waldar had put together. I'd told them to pick twenty of their best, but only so I could see the options. I'd have my own criteria for the strike team.

"What's the plan?" Waldar asked as we headed in the direction of the clearing. I was pretty sure it was one of the areas we'd patrolled yesterday, but wanted another look at the size.

I bit back a half laugh. "We don't actually have time for a plan. Not a proper one." I shrugged. "So, we'll do what they say. We'll even load the ore for them, make up some sort of nonsense about how delicate it is."

Which made me wonder. "You said Volsh and his crew shouldn't have known the location of the settlement, what you're working on here. Any possibility they would know about the cyprtite itself? Stability, properties, anything?"

"They shouldn't." The older man drew his eyebrows together. "But you're right, we can't count on that."

"It's the only way I can imagine for us to get on that ship. And that's where we need to go."

"Why would they risk having us on board?" Therra asked as we arrived at the clearing.

"People like that think they're above any sort of manual labor." I answered as my eyes ran over the size of the clearing, the surrounding tree line, guessed how solid the ground might be under the snow.

"If they can get their ship down in this amount of space, and they're not worried about sinking to their bellies in mud and snow melt, then the intel is probably right. Crew of five, maybe six. Seven would be pushing it in a ship of that size."

A muscle jumped in Waldar's jaw, and I put my hand on his shoulder. The information was from the missing girl, but he had to put that away if we were going to get through the next hour.

"Our only chance is a team of our best fighters loading the crates into their hold. They won't be expecting any resistance, not after Volsh's display. But it's a harsh world out on the fringe. If they've survived this long, they're not stupid. Chances are good their entire crew will have their guns on us."

Therra nodded. "Would they keep the pilot on the bridge?"

"They might," I thought. I would. One on the bridge, ready to clear out at the first sign of Imperials. One standing guard over the girl, if she was still alive, and the rest supervising the loading of the ore. If it was a bigger crew, I'd put a few in the settlement, take more hostages to ensure the good behavior of the loaders.

But for proper coverage, they wouldn't have enough people for that. Good, one less complication to worry about.

I took another look at the possible members of the team. Evenly mixed between men and women, all of them held themselves easily. They'd good in a fight. Waldar swore they were dead shots and not afraid to throw a punch, mix it up.

But, that was never all there was to it.

"How many of you have kids?" I called out.

A number of hands rose.

"There's no guarantees any of us will get off that ship."

A woman snapped, "My kids are the reason I want to fight. We'll all fight harder, knowing what we've got to lose."

I couldn't argue with that.

"How many of you have ever killed before?"

They all shook their heads. Made sense, I supposed, a small community like this, and everyone seemed pretty close knit. But it made me nervous.

"That's what the business is. We're going in there to kill. If you've got the slightest problem with that, now's the time to back out."

Waldar and Therra had picked well. Not one of them turned away.

In the end, I picked five, a team of six, including me. If I thought we could get more on without raising any flags, I would've.

"The rest of you fade out into the trees, find a nest, keep your rifles close. There's a chance they'll try to make a break for it off the ship. Don't let them get away."

Waldar pulled me aside. "Why am I not on the team," he growled. "I may be old, but I'm not useless. My children are grown, less to lose."

Void. Nothing in my training prepared me to be tactful, but, for the first time, I wished I had a bit more of that skill. "Because I need you elsewhere," I hissed. "I can't have Therra worried about you, and you've said yourself she's a better shot."

His eyes narrowed, but he didn't say anything. I cast around for more reasons to keep him off the strike team. "Besides, I need you back in town keeping everyone's heads down. People will listen to you. I don't know, can't trust that from anyone else."

"That's bull-"

His words were cut off by the crew bringing the final load of crates to the edge of the clearing.

Just behind them, Eris came running up, her hands full. Hyso slouched beside her, considerably more at ease. I don't know what it was about the other mech, but he set my teeth on edge.

She had a grin pasted on her face, but her eyes looked worried. "It's the best I can come up with in the time we've got. Six magnetic broadcast devices and a master switch. Should scramble their nav solid."

She scanned the clearing and I could see her working out angles and deployment in her head. "Volsh picked a good location for us. There's no way they can land here and not be in range."

Eris handed half the devices to the boy next to her, pointing out spots in the tree line at the far side of the clearing. He dashed off, eager to do his job. I noticed she kept the other three to place herself and didn't give them to Hyso.

Eris and the boy returned at nearly the same time. They found me while I was going over the cache of weapons the colonists had gathered. Mostly plasma rifles, too long for what I had planned, but there were enough short-range blasters and phasers to work.

I motioned for the extra empty crates I'd asked for and started stowing weapons inside in pairs.

Eris held the master switch, rocking a little from side to side. I recognized the nervous energy building - ready for a fight, waiting for it, wishing it would get here just to be over it.

"They shouldn't notice anything until they try to lift off." She flashed an evil grin. Then they'll have their hands full. I'll stay, monitor and set it off manually, if need be."

At her words ice curled in my belly. After everything I had said to the team, I knew I was a hypocrite. But no matter what happened, I couldn't stand to have her this close to whatever went down on the ship.

I shook my head. "You and the kid have another job. Whatever happens here, that refiner needs to be fixed. Letting it get used for scrap was part of what got them into this mess. Get it sorted."

Her eyes narrowed and I could tell I was in for it.

"Then who do you think is going to spring the trap? I don't

notice you having a surplus of techs hanging around." She threw her hands up in disgust. "How much trouble do you think I'm going to get into back in the tree line?"

We had minutes before the ship was due to arrive, no time to fight fair. I nodded towards the kid who stood back a few feet, but his eyes were fixed on her.

"What about him? You know perfectly well, if you stay, so does he."

Her jaw tightened, and I could see the arguments marshaling behind her eyes. Then her figure slumped, defeated. "Damn you. That's a dirty strike."

I pulled her into my arms and, for just a second, gave myself the luxury of breathing in her scent, burying my face in her hair.

"But you know it's true," I murmured in her ear.

A gruff cough interrupted us. "I can take care of it. I shadowed the ship's maintenance officer of the colony ship on the transit out." Waldar shrugged. "Not enough background to build something like this, but I'm at least capable of making sure it gets set off. Neva, Petro's widow, can take care of things in town." He shot me a look as if daring me to argue. "Nobody's going to give her any problems right now."

Eris handed the detonator to Waldar, and gave him a few brief instructions.

"Come on, Kel," she slung her arm over the kid's shoulders. "We can tell we're not wanted here."

They headed back through the trees, back to what I hoped would be relative safety in the settlement. As she crossed the tree line, Eris glanced over her shoulder, caught me watching her. Our eyes met, and she smiled, threw back her shoulders. When she disappeared into the trees, I swore I could almost hear her talking about gears and set times and ratios to the kid.

She'd do her job, time for me to do mine. I checked the chrono. Minutes left.

"Alright, everyone, let's get ready." I tapped the crates one by one, group by group. "We'll start with these, two to a crate. Handle them as if your sleeping newborn child is curled up inside, got it?"

"Ummm," one of the guys interrupted. "The ore isn't really that volatile."

The woman who'd spoke up before, Raz, I remembered now, elbowed him in the side. "Yeah, but they don't know that."

Glad that she'd handled things, I went on with the plan, such as it was.

"We'll get this group of three in, then the next batch. Let the crew see we're just doing our job. We can look plenty unhappy, but we're obviously not there to give them any trouble." I grinned. "Let's give them time to get relaxed."

I moved down the line of crates. "On the third load, that's our surprise."

I cracked the lid of the crate I stood next to now, so that they all could see the weapons hidden within.

One of the strike team grinned with an almost feral look in his eyes, and I knew we'd picked the right people.

The high whine of breaking atmosphere made everyone flinch. At a quick gesture from Therra, the rest of the settlement faded back into the trees. It was just our band of six now.

The ship circled, and then hovered above the clearing, slowly lowering a battered hull to the ground. From the looks of the ship, they hadn't had an easy time of things. Eris would know better, but, even to my untrained eye, there were badly done repairs and probably delayed maintenance that would end up costing them. Finding a defenseless settlement with riches just waiting to be picked up must have seemed like a dream.

It'd be my job to turn that into a nightmare.

They touched down and, in minutes, the belly opened up, a platform descending towards the ground. Two of the outlaw crew stood on the deck, weapons drawn and faces grim.

"Let's do this thing." I bent towards the first crate.

ERIS

My eyes darted from one thing to the next in the shop. It was harder than I could've imagined to get my mind back to the task of rebuilding the parts we needed to restore the refiner.

I went to the data center, pulled up the plans we'd worked out yesterday. They might as well have been random squiggles on the screen, for all my focus.

I chewed my lip, flicked the schematics off and began another scan for Nixie's signal, desperate for something, anything, to distract me.

But no matter how I patterned the search, the result was the same. Still nothing. So be it.

I sighed and pulled the schematics back up. One, two, maybe three, more sections to build out before we'd be able to test our work.

I tapped it, expanded the first section.

Hyso looked over. "Yeah, we can work that through. Should take most of the day." He glanced over at me, eyes narrowed. "What do you think is happening now?"

I flicked my eyes towards Kel and shook my head minutely.

Not the time or the place for my fears. "I'm sure everything's going to work out fine."

Kel looked at me, eyes wide. His mother, as a medic, wasn't on the attack team but, instead, had been placed within the tree line, ready to take care of any injured.

"Do you think they'll get her back?" he asked. From the glimpse I'd had of the girl held hostage, it seemed likely that Kel and Aggie had been friends.

I had been hoping he wouldn't ask. It was one thing for adults to decide there was no choice but to risk the life of one child to save the rest. It was entirely another to have to justify that decision to that child's friend.

"They're going to do the best they can."

He frowned. "How good is that, exactly?"

Definitely an engineer in the making. "Connor is very good at fighting. And I know the people he would have picked to fight beside him would also be very good."

He picked up a sonic spanner from the bench, fidgeted with it in his hands. "Is he better than Therra is?"

"Is Therra the best hunter here?"

He didn't look up from the workbench, just nodded.

"I think Connor is probably better for this sort of fighting. He's had more experience off planet, for one thing. I don't expect Therra has had a lot of times she's had to fight against other people here."

Kel shook his head. "No, that wouldn't really be our way."

I gestured for the expanded schematic of section one to appear on the wall screen, zoomed and rotated it until we could see inside.

"See how all of our measurements from yesterday have paid off? Now we can see what we're going to be doing."

His eyes roamed the diagram, but he stayed silent.

"You can bet that they'll be planning just the same with their attack on the shuttle."

Kel's face finally cleared, just a bit. "So, that will make it easier once they attack?"

"I'm sure it will," I said, hoping my voice sounded steadier than my heartbeat.

I thought about Connor, thought about his arms wrapped around me at the edge of the clearing. For a moment, I felt the slightest brush against my mind, like the wing of a moth.

My confusion must've shown on my face, because Hyso looked at me sharply. "What?"

"Nothing." I shook my head.

I forced my attention back to the plans. "Let's get back to work".

CONNOR

The first two rounds of loading the crates went as smoothly as planned. In pairs, we'd lifted the boxes, shuffled slowly over to the lowered platform under the watchful eyes of the bandits. Two had remained on the platform at all times, a man and a woman.

On the first load, as the platform raised us into the belly of the cargo bay, I kept my head down but slowly tilted to use the most of my peripheral vision.

As I expected, Volsh and an additional crew member were stationed inside the cargo bay, both with weapons trained on the platform, in case of any unexpected surprises being raised into the ship.

"Get a move on," Volsh barked.

"Don't want us to move too fast, boss," Raz answered, easing her crate around a corner with her partner. "Cyprtite needs gentle handling."

He backed up slightly, his weapon never wavering. "How do we know it's not going to blow?"

"We want the girl back, that's all," Raz kept her voice smooth and soft, even as she and her partner moved their assigned crate.

"Everything is packed and padded, just don't want to give anything a jolt."

The rest of his crew split their attention between us and Volsh, waiting for his orders.

Volsh stalked over, eyes narrowed with suspicion.

"I'm not going to put up with anyone playing games," he spat.

"Really, we don't-"

"Shut up!" he barked, and wrenched open the crate Therra and I held.

"Looks padded enough to take a few bumps," he muttered, then stalked away, while we both eased out slow breaths.

As we grunted and moved the crates into the designated corner, I took the chance to look around.

Again, I wished Eris could see the ship. Under the sloppy repairs and careless patching, I saw good lines. Maybe the ship's crew had fallen on hard times. Or maybe they just didn't care.

There was little other cargo in the hold. Either they'd just finished a round of trades, and their accounts were fat with credits, or whatever deals the gang had hoped to make had fallen through.

Recent success could make them careless. Desperation, more dangerous.

Returning to the platform, I scanned for any cameras or other monitoring devices. I saw four, but three looked to be broken, only one active. The crew looked well fed enough, clothing looked new and studded with gaudy trinkets. And they all had the flat eyes of killers.

It seemed safe to assume that, even with credits in hand, they just didn't care enough about basic maintenance to make it high-priority.

As our team left the lowered platform and moved towards the third batch of crates, I paused.

"What?" Therra looked at me warily, ready for a change in plan.

I shook my head, wanting to recapture the sense of it, but it was gone.

The feeling of Eris next to me, so strongly I could almost scent her. But that wasn't the sort of thing you wanted to hear from your partner right before a firefight.

"Nothing," I answered.

"Better not be," she shrugged. "No time."

We hefted the box together. "Need to have your head in the game."

"It's never been anything but," I muttered.

I studied the rest of the team. They'd held up better than I'd expected from civilians. Some tension, some waiting for the fight to start. But solid.

Just as we had the previous two times, we carefully loaded the set of crates onto the platform.

At this point, the guards looked bored with the whole process. They'd seen what we wanted them to - cowed, submissive settlers, doing what they demanded.

I caught Raz's eyes, and then looked at the two guards on the platform.

She nodded, tapped a finger fractionally on her crate to signal her partner.

The final pair on the team, dark-haired brothers or cousins, glanced above us into the hold with raised eyebrows. I blinked, slowly. Their targets would be the guards waiting for us inside.

Therra and I would split off, providing cover for the other teams, and taking our best shots as we could find them. Once the hold was secured, we'd fan through the ship in pairs, searching for the girl.

As long as Eris' device worked, they'd be grounded, unable to flee.

But I knew how quickly she'd had to build it. She wouldn't have had time to test it. Even with Waldar babysitting it, we'd need to move fast.

As we maneuvered the third load of crates into place, I glanced up, met Therra's eyes.

Go time.

We flipped the decoy crate over as a shield and grabbed the weapons that spilled out.

The two other teams performed the same maneuver, their own crates providing some cover while they started picking off their targets.

Volsh bellowed in rage, then ran behind a bulwark near the stairs leading out of the cargo bay.

He froze, as Therra patiently pinged the hull next to him, effectively pinning him.

Raz grazed her target and swore, took a deep breath, and calibrated with precision and fatal results.

One of the bandits made what must've seemed like a clever decision, slapping the button to lower the loading platform. The instant she had enough clearance, she wiggled out, dropping to the ground below.

The sizzle of a plasma rifle, and a sharply cut off scream let me know the snipers in the tree line had done their work.

Ten seconds and two down, two left.

The brothers had cornered the last man behind a pile of scrap. I turned my attention to Therra. She'd kept Volsh from escaping by placing shots every time he tried to squirm out from behind the bulwark. Ideally, we'd take him alive. It'd keep us from having to scour the entire ship for the girl, and, with enough persuasion, we could find out how many other bandits knew about the colony's secret mining operation.

I moved wide of her stream of fire, placing myself between Volsh and the stairway out of the cargo bay. I let myself settle into the rhythm of the battle, the pattern in the seemingly random bursts of fire, waiting for my chance to tackle Volsh.

A frenzied scream echoed from the permisteel walls, jerking my attention back. A man leapt from a catwalk, blaster aimed towards the brothers' backs. Time slowed down, movements playing like a vid. One of the brothers began to turn, recognizing the threat, but it was clear they wouldn't make it in time.

I spun, firing as I hurdled crates. One blast caught the attacker in the chest, slamming him back against the wall.

The brothers stood over him, gasping.

"Must have had a hidey hole back there, a way up to the rigging," one heaved, nudging the body.

"Shit!" Therra yelled behind me.

Volsh had taken advantage of our distraction to take a shot at her. Blood streamed from between her fingers where she clutched at her arm. The clatter of the metal treads told me Volsh was somewhere up above.

I sprinted back across the hold. "Go after him," she griped. "My own fault for looking away."

A quick glance showed me the wound was minor. Raz knelt down next to Therra. "Easy fix. We've got her."

I tore up the stairs after Volsh. At the top, a thick hatch lowered, already down to knee height. I dove, rolling under it just before it crashed down.

On the other side of the hatch I heard the brothers pounding the controls, but, at first guess, Volsh had fried it.

Try to open it, and have a backup?

No time.

At the end of the passageway I saw a flicker of shadow, and I took off after it. The passageway was eerily silent, other than that pounding of our feet against the metal floors.

A scorch burned deep into my shoulder and I cursed myself. Volsh had dodged into a side passageway, waiting for me to cross, framed as an easy shot like a picture.

Unfortunately for him, it just pissed me off.

Damage was minor, nothing my internal systems couldn't repair, faster if I stopped and let them, but it would do well enough even while still on the hunt.

I accelerated down the side passageway towards him, and had the pleasure of watching his eyes go wide with fright, just for a moment.

He turned and ran, screaming as he went, "Systems on! Start the engines, get out of here!"

"Acknowledged," sounded from the speakers. But the voice was cold, mechanical. An AI pilot, at best. That would simplify my life.

The thrum of the engines filled the ship, then sputtered and died. Another attempt at lift, and a shudder shook the passageway as we settled more firmly into the earth.

Way to go, babe. Eris would be pleased her contraption had held.

I closed the gap between us with every step, but still he remained maddeningly just out of reach.

He twisted down another passageway, sliding down a ladder and then dashing off again. What was he doing? This wasn't the way to the bridge. Was he just hoping to lose me somewhere in the bowels of the ship?

I had my answer soon enough.

Volsh stood in a small room, gasping for air. I could see where some of Therra's shots had grazed him. Good.

But his blaster wasn't pointed at me, rather at the cryo pod on the wall next to him.

"Drop your weapon, or the girl dies."

The chamber was tilted at enough of an angle that I could see through the swirling mist within.

It was the same girl we'd seen at the shuttle.

My blaster fell to the floor with a clatter, and I sagged against the hatch, letting my hand go up to my shoulder where I'd been hit, covering any ongoing repairs from a casual glance.

"Thought I took you more squarely than that." Volsh frowned. "Maybe it was a low charge."

His eyes narrowed. "Kick the blaster this way."

At my hesitation, he gestured again towards the girl in the cryo pod. "I don't care if the girl lives or dies. Apparently, you do."

I could see his finger tighten on the trigger.

"Give a guy a chance to get his breath, you got me good back there." I pushed up from the frame of the door, staggered a bit. It was mostly for show.

Mostly.

"Coming over." I caught the toe of my boot under the muzzle of the blaster and, with one sharp kick, sent it spinning towards Volsh's face.

Instinctively, he ducked, and I dove and rolled to the other side of the room, drawing his fire away from the cryo pod.

There wasn't much cover in the room. Looked like a badly stocked medbay. I grabbed a rolling tray of instruments and flung it at Volsh, looking for a better weapon. His shots went wild through the room and he yelled, "I'm going to kill you, kill the girl, and then kill you again."

Gauze and adhesives went flying as I pulled out drawers, throwing them after a brief glance.

Finally, he got smart. "Freeze, or I take her out."

He was right. I wasn't going to find another weapon, not a makeshift cutter or reasonably sized blade.

Which left one option.

I dove towards him. He swung his blaster up from the girl, but not before I wrapped my hand around his neck.

His eyes bulged as I squeezed, and his knees collapsed. As we fell to the floor, he squirmed in a final, desperate maneuver, jamming his blaster between us.

Damn, that hurt.

I twisted as I fell back, the ray catching my side but good. He stood panting above me, face red with fury.

"I'm going to kill you, kill the girl, then waste this entire backwater."

"Seems like a bit of an overreaction, don't you think?" All I wanted to do was fade out into the comfortable black, but, if I failed here, everyone was at risk, Eris was at risk.

I tried to move. Side hurt, arm hurt, back hurt... wait. When did my back get hit? I needed more time. "Seriously, if you look at it right, you got what you came for, and now you don't have to share with your crew."

If possible, he got even redder, but my wandering mind kept being distracted by the thing digging into my spine. I stretched my good arm around, and fought a flicker of a smile.

"That's it, you son of a bitch," Volsh snarled. "You might have thought you were protecting those dirt grubbers, but you've signed their death warrant."

"Maybe," I sighed, then pulled my blaster from behind me, where I'd fallen on it in our scuffle. He fired, and I took him out as cleanly as he'd killed Petro.

"But maybe not."

As his body hit the floor, I staggered to the cryo pod and slapped the revival sequence into place.

As I slumped down against the wall, I heard the hiss of the pod lid cycling open.

"Better hope they get that hatch door open soon, kid," I muttered, then closed my eyes.

ERIS

*U*sually it doesn't take long for me to get into the flow of working on a project. Today, it just wouldn't come. Every minute I caught myself checking the chrono, wondering what was happening on the ship.

Every minute I had to drag my attention back to what I was supposed to be doing.

Finally, Hyso threw down his tools in disgust. "This is such a waste of time. I'm going to do something else until you get your head together."

"Don't you even care about them? Your friends are fighting, too." I snapped, angry with myself, but his baffling attitude gave me a good distraction.

"No, they're just the people who live in the settlement with me," he spat out from a side bench where he slouched, scrolling through panels of parallel screens.

Okay…. I stopped. "Hey, do you have outward connection again?"

He flicked the tablet off again. "No, that was saved from before. I said I'd tell you when communications were back on, didn't I?"

That was weirdly defensive, but before I could figure my way back onto safe conversational ground, Neva burst through the door.

"Eris, come with me, quickly," she gasped.

I threw down my tools. "What is it?" My heart stopped, just for a moment. "Is Connor..." I couldn't finish.

"No," she shook her head. "At least, we don't know. But Volsh closed the hatch to the rest of the ship and damaged the panel. We can't get it open."

Neva's face was full of anguish. "We don't know what's going on with Connor, or Aggie."

Right, then. An engineering issue I could handle.

"Let me get tools," I turned back to the bench, searching for what I'd need.

"Hurry," she pleaded, but I kept looking. If he fried the lock, without the right equipment, it wouldn't matter when I got there.

"Hyso, I'm going to borrow-"

"Sure, take what you need."

Whatever. I'd deal with Mister Mood Swings later. Or never. I didn't really have time to care right now.

I grabbed an armful of things that might be useful. Kel picked up the pieces I dropped.

"Let's go."

When I came to the hatchway at the top of the stairs, my heart sank. In their attempts to unfreeze the mechanism, someone had enthusiastically gone about hacking their way through the wall plate with whatever tools were at hand.

"Excuse me", I said, pushing my way through the crowd a little more brusquely than I should have. But if they had damaged the mechanism, it was going to make it harder to get this thing up and out of the way.

I spread the tools out in front of me and blocked everything but the project at hand from my mind.

"We need to get through faster than that," a man said. "We

don't know what's going on."

I tuned him out, even as Neva hushed him.

"If you could have gotten through, you would've done it by now. Let her do her work."

And then the room faded away, their voices silencing as I let my mind slip through, imagining the mechanism as I knew it must have been, seeing where the fault was, why the hatch wasn't working. For a moment, I missed Nixie, but shoved it away.

"There," I breathed.

My hands reached for the tools, flying back and forth between the wall and the hatch, a little here, a little more there.

Finally, I joined two wires together and held my breath.

With the screech of protesting gears, the hatch slid upwards.

Maybe not my best work, but it would do for now.

I started to wiggle through the opening, but Therra, her arm bandaged I now noticed, held me back.

"We don't know what's on the other side, wait. Let the fighters go first."

"The hell with that," I snapped and turned back to the hatchway. Tears of frustration filled my eyes and I pushed away from Therra as the door finished rolling upwards.

A long passageway opened up, and, at the end, I could see two figures, one large, one small. They were moving towards us. I tensed. Was Volsh relying on his hostage to get out of here?

I blinked, clearing my eyes. Not Volsh. I ran towards Connor and the girl. Dark red stained more of Connor's jacket than I wanted to think about, and he leaned heavily against the girl.

Aggie's eyes were large, but any confusion she felt was swept away when her mother rushed past me in the passageway and gathered her in her arms.

Connor leaned against the wall with his eyes closed. I slid next to him, trying to keep my voice light. "Come on," I gently pulled his arm over my shoulder. "I'll make a better crutch anyway."

He grinned, and together we hobbled back down the

passageway.

"How badly are you hurt?" I asked in a whisper, as if saying the words aloud would somehow make his injuries worse.

"Nothing I can't deal with, nothing I haven't dealt with before."

"Oh."

Sion met us at the top of the stairs. "It looks like Aggie's going to be okay, can't say the same about you."

"Looks like they kept her in a cryo pod most of the time. Probably the safest place for her," Connor grunted.

He eyed the stairs warily then braced his shoulders and started down.

Sion rolled her eyes. "You obviously took a couple of hits. Let me take a look at you, get you fixed up."

I followed Connor down the stairs and tried to cover for him as he caught his breath.

A tiny fear gripped my heart.

I'd never seen him out of breath.

Granted, we hadn't known each other long, but certainly in the time we had known each other, enough things had happened that should have caused him to lose his breath.

But he hadn't.

Until now.

Connor shrugged. "It's not mine, must be the other guy's. I'm just bruised. Just going to sleep it off."

Sion frowned, but, although I could feel her eyes drilling holes in my back as we lowered the platform to the ground below, she didn't say anything further.

"Are you really going to be fine?" I couldn't help asking when we were out of earshot.

"Will be. But I could really use a nap." He squeezed my shoulder. "And the shower. I hate the way blood feels when it dries on me."

"It wasn't the other guy's blood, was it?"

"No," he admitted. "But you can't blame me for not wanting to let a medtek get any closer to me than necessary."

"Connor," I said with some exasperation, "these people are on our side."

"No, we were on their side. When it comes down to it, we don't really know that much about them, how closely tied to the Empire they are."

I said nothing, my eyes fixed on the ground, listening to his breathing, feeling the warmth of his body next to mine.

"Alright, I promise." he said heavily. "Let's get to the cabin, let me get cleaned up some. If you still think I need to go see her, I will."

"Really?" I looked up, feeling a little better that he wasn't going to be such a baby about seeing the doctor.

"Yes." Connor's eyes twinkled. "But only if you help me wash my back."

As we reached the cabin, Connor's steps slowed.

"Why don't you go to the workshop for a couple of hours," he said. "It's going to take me a while to clean up, then all I'm going to be good for is sleep."

Inside I screamed with frustration but, instead, I helped him up the stairs and through the door.

He leaned one shoulder against the wall, and I noticed he was careful to keep the bloody areas of the jacket away from the interior of our borrowed home.

I shed my coat and moved to undo the fastenings on his before he could stop me.

"You're out of your mind, if you think that after all of that wondering and waiting I'm going to be put off by a little blood."

"It might be more than a little."

"If it is, then you promised to let me get Sion. What's the problem?"

He rolled his eyes, but didn't fight when I eased the jacket off his shoulders.

The layers of shirts got bloodier the further we went. When I got to the thin undershirt, he grabbed my wrist.

"Let me."

I raised my eyebrows. "I haven't noticed you complaining that I've hurt you yet."

He had winced once or twice as I maneuvered around his wounded shoulder, but that had been all.

"Are you hiding more secrets?"

"Not from you." He let out a deep breath, shoulders unwinding.

"Then let's get this done."

I pulled it off and fought down my gasp. His abdomen was covered with blood, no more than I'd been expecting from the condition of his shirts, but somehow it was a surprise to see so much of it against his skin.

Except...

"None of it looks damp anymore."

"Wouldn't expect it to be. I'd be in much worse shape if I was still bleeding."

"Let's get you rinsed off, see what's underneath."

He stood there, the shadow of a cocky grin twisting his lips. "You're not going to help me out of my pants?"

I laughed. "Now I know you're fine."

Once we'd both skinned down and gotten into the shower, the knot around my heart loosened. The skin at his injured shoulder and abdomen was smooth, unbroken, just an angry red.

"Yep, that would be a hard one to explain."

The water rushed over us both and I closed my eyes, luxuriating in the feeling of unlimited water.

I let my mind wander. The danger was over, we were both all right, and maybe, just maybe, I could barter for Volsh's ship. Once I found Nixie, all would be right with the world.

Broad hands slid around me from behind, cupping my breasts.

I leaned back into Connors's chest and relaxed. "You did say a shower would make you feel better."

He leaned over, and kissed the top of my shoulder, then worked his way up to the hollow below my ear.

I groaned and turned, going soft in his hands as the liquid heat his touch ignited in my core melted through me.

I wrapped my arms around his neck, stretching up on my toes to kiss him long and hard.

His hand slid down my back, fingers kneading into the curve of my ass, pulling me closer into him. Strong hands lifted me, wrapping below my thighs until my back was against the shower wall, legs wrapped around his hips.

"I want you now, Eris," he growled in my ear.

I curled my fingers into his shoulders as I pulled him in for another kiss.

And I felt him wince at my touch.

My eyes snapped open. I saw where my hand gripped onto his wounded shoulder.

"Void, I'm sorry."

I wiggled, and felt the hard length of him under me.

"Connor, let me down."

Reluctantly he lowered me to the floor, a scowl on his face.

I shut off the water and handed him a towel, then began to dry myself off while he stood unmoving.

"You can't tell me you're healed enough for bed games when me holding your shoulder makes you flinch."

"Got distracted," he muttered. I wrapped my towel around myself and went to cup his face in my hands.

"I promise we'll finish this. Let's get you healed first, and then I'm all yours." I brushed wet hair out of his smoldering eyes. "Or you're all mine. Either way."

"Something always happens. Meteors, pirates, something." He dried off, still in a cranky mood.

"Are you hungry?"

Connor's shoulders sagged. "Ravenous." He grinned wryly.

"And if thoughts of food can distract me from what we were doing, you're right, I need to heal more."

Apparently, Connor had been watching Waldar closely during their visit last night, because dinner was actually edible.

"That settles it," I said as I picked up our plates from the table. "You're on cooking duty from here out. I'll handle the dishes."

He was silent and I realized his eyes had drifted half closed. I ran my hands over his muscled back, careful this time to avoid the still healing shoulder.

"Go to bed. I'll be right there. Plenty of time to figure our next steps in the morning."

When I slid in after him, his arm curled around me, pulling me into his warm body, and we both floated into sleep.

The nightmare began as it always did.

I wandered alone at the fields on the outskirts of my family's ranch. The air was hot and heavy.

I'd run out to hide from the terrible, wandering hands of my uncle. I couldn't have been any more than five or six, but, still, I knew staying in the house wasn't safe.

Out here, in this far pasture, I could see nothing but open, rolling hills. Not even trees tall enough to break the horizon line as far as I could see.

I trampled down the dry, late summer grass and curled up to watch the tiny creatures all around. I'd overheard my grandfather talking about selling the ranch, one of the last large spreads. We'd be rich, but I hated the thought of leaving.

Here I was safe.

Here, no one could find me.

Until the soft raindrops of an afternoon storm hardened and became biting hail then the shriek of the wind wasn't loud enough to drown my cries.

The sheltering grass turned into a thousand whips, cutting my tender skin.

Dark, roiling clouds filled the sky, and I whimpered with every flash and crack of lightning.

And it was always the same.

Nowhere to run, nowhere to hide, nowhere out of sight of the threatening deadly sky.

"Come back to me, Eris." The whisper was just barely audible over the noise of the storm. "Honey, you're so cold."

Lightning exploded next to me, charging the air with the burnt taste of electricity.

The voice was insistent now. "Wake up!"

With a gasp, I sat up in bed, shaking uncontrollably.

Connor lifted me into his lap, wrapped his arms around my shivering body, and tucked my head under his chin.

"I'm okay," I gasped. "I'm okay, it was just a dream."

"I don't care what it was, you're staying here until you're warm."

I nestled into his chest, breathing in his clean scent, pushing away the last clinging remnants of the nightmare.

His hands stroked my back, warming and calming, and, as I relaxed, I could feel something else poking me from below.

I shifted. "Sorry, that can't be comfortable."

He ran his fingers through my hair, and I shivered, pulled by a different tension now. "There's always something we could do about it."

The skin of his abdomen still felt raw to me, but he pushed my hand aside, turned me until my back curved into his chest. "I'm fine, I promise."

Connor's mouth fell on the side of my neck, and my only answer was a low groan, tilting my head back to give him better access.

His hands wrapped around my front, one kneading and flicking my swollen nipples, the other caressing down towards the juncture of my legs.

He pinched the other nipple, and lightning sparked inside me, arching my back into him.

But this lightning I didn't fear. I craved his touch, begged for more.

His arms tightened around me, restricting my movements, until I could only squirm and gasp at the onslaught of his mouth and hands.

A short scream escaped me as one thick finger slid between my lower lips, teasing and tracing around my clit.

"Connor, please," I whimpered, aching to push myself into him, but held still by his iron grip.

"Anything you ask," he whispered, and ran his tongue around the shell of my ear.

With excruciating deliberation, first one finger, then another pumped inside me and I shattered, the pressure of sensation expelling the breath from my body.

I began to float back down, only for him to grind the heel of his palm into my mound as he drove into me again.

The touch of his teeth at my throat set me on fire, and I thrashed in his arms, defenseless against the waves of pleasure igniting my nerves.

Somehow, eventually, I was cradled against his chest again, breathing hard as if I'd run down all the corridors of the *Daedalus* twice over.

"Back with me?" Connor kissed the top of my head. Even that lightest of touches sent an aftershock through my body.

"Mmmm," I answered, and this time when I squirmed to turn around in his arms, he let me.

"We still haven't done anything about this, you know." I wrapped my fingers around the length of him. If anything, he was harder, thicker now.

"What did you have in mind?" I felt rather than saw his grin in the darkness, and tilted my head up to press my lips against his.

His tongue flicked against the seam of my lips, and I opened to him, even as I trailed my fingers to his root and back to the weeping head. This time it was his turn to groan against me, his voice going deeper with every stroke.

I slid until I knelt over him, barely brushing his cock with my cunt. I tilted his head towards me until I could whisper. "I want you in me." I nipped at his earlobe. "Now."

With a roar, he grabbed my hips and slammed me down over his cock, spearing me, splitting me in two.

His arms trembled, holding me in place. "Are you alright?" he managed between gritted teeth.

"Give me a moment to adjust," I panted, squirming. He curled his fingers into my hips as a reflexive twitch hit me.

"Be careful doing that," he growled. "I can't be held responsible."

"Oh, really."

The next twitch was definitely on purpose, and his paper-thin control tore in two.

I grabbed his chest for balance as he lifted and pounded into me, faster and faster until all I could feel was him, us, the points we connected.

With a smooth twist, he rolled us until he was on top, never slowing his pace. "Open your eyes, Eris," he commanded, startling me. I'd been so lost to sensation I didn't know when I'd closed them.

The intensity on his face pushed me to the edge again, just as surely as his touch. I wrapped my arms around his neck, pulling his mouth to mine. "Come with me, come with me," I coaxed, and, with his eyes locked on mine, we splintered into the darkness, my screams tangled with his shouts.

Exhausted, we curled together until the chill had me scrambling for the covers.

Safe, we're both safe, I thought hazily as I drifted off.

"Planning to keep you that way," he murmured. "Even from the storm."

Then we both submerged into sleep once more.

~

IN THE MORNING, I woke before Connor. He shrugged back under the covers, and I tucked the quilts around him, brushing back the spikes of his dark blond hair.

"Rest up," I dropped a kiss on his forehead, and he smiled slightly in his sleep. "Tomorrow may be busy."

My thoughts spun, full and happy, on the way to Hyso's workshop. Maybe, with Volsh's ship, we could run a better search for Nixie's signature. And once the mag storm finally passed, I could pull some banked credits, see what sort of deal we could work for the ship. Maybe everything was going to work out after all.

"Heya," I waved to Hyso as I came through the workshop doors. "I'm just going to do another scan before we get started on the refiner, alright?"

I punched in the parameters, paying half-attention to Hyso moving behind me.

"What was that?" I turned, then froze.

Hyso's face was a mask of fury, but what scared me more was the blaster pointed at me.

"It's all your fault. You and that weird guy had to come, screw everything up. You owe me."

"Wait!" But there was only blackness.

CONNOR

I woke up and stretched, checking for any pull of muscles in my shoulder or gut. Still a little tender, would've been better to have been back in the medbay on the *Daedelus*. But if I was there, I wouldn't have Eris.

Her side of the bed was cold, and I had a hazy memory of her slipping out earlier this morning.

Probably checking over that ship, seeing what she could do to get us off this planet and back into space.

In the shower, I thought about Doc's hidden accounts. I always knew she had backup of funds, "little cushions," she always called them. I'd come across a file of codes once, figured out what they were for pretty fast.

Never needed them before, but, if a simple lack of funds was all that stood between Eris and that ship, I could make that go away.

Just as soon as this magnetic storm was over.

I dressed, musing. I'd never heard of a magnetic storm this intense, or running this long. Either something was weird with this solar system's patterns, or someone was lying.

After a half-hearted brush at the bloodstains, I pulled on the jacket anyway.

Or, knowing the nature of people, some mixture of the strange and lies.

Stepping out onto the porch of the cabin, I saw the kid Eris had been working with yesterday across the street.

"Hey," I waved and trotted down the stairs. "I'm heading to the ship, find Eris. You want to come?"

His eyes widened. "My mom said I wasn't supposed to go explore it, but," he trailed off and, by the gleam in his eyes, I wondered why anyone had ever had the notion that children were innocent. "It's entirely different if I'm with you and Eris, right?"

"Sure." A slight urge towards responsibility hit me. "Did the rest of the adults sweep through it yesterday after I left, just in case we missed any of the gang?"

The kid, Kel I finally remembered, turned and trotted after me. "Sure they did, they were looking for people, and probably extra supplies. We do pretty well here, but it would be stupid to turn down stuff when it falls in your lap."

Practical kid. I liked that.

I cleared my throat. "How's the girl doing, Aggie?"

He was silent for a long while. "Mom says she's fine, said somehow she slept through the whole thing." He looked up at me, brows pulled together. "When I went to talk to her, it was almost like she didn't recognize me, didn't know where she was."

I put my hand on his shoulder. "Well, there might be a couple things going on. If they didn't adjust the cryo-chamber for a child, she may have gotten more of the sleepy chemicals then she should have for someone her age. It might take her a while to knock that out of her system. And the other, well, sometimes when really scary things happen, your mind has a way of sort of shutting down, building a wall around it."

I thought about Eris, that open field in the storm.

"You're going to be a good friend to her, right?"

He nodded, eyes solemn.

"Then you just wait, be patient, and keep being her friend. She'll be around soon enough".

Thankfully, at this point we reached the edge of the clearing, and the ship distracted Kel from any further serious talk.

The loading platform was down, and I could hear voices up in the cargo bay.

Eris' scent was faint, she hadn't been here since yesterday, I was sure. But just to check…

"Hail the ship," I called up and Raz' face emerged from the edge of the bay.

"Hey there," she called down. "You're looking better than I expected you'd be. Hang on, I'll bring you up."

"No need," I answered. "Just wanted to see if Eris had been by yet."

She shook her head. "Haven't seen her all morning."

Well, there was only one other place I'd imagine she'd be. I looked down at my short companion.

"I know I promised we could explore the ship, but, first, can you show me the way to Hyso's workshop?"

Probably I could follow her scent there, but, with all the mixed paths of the other residents crossing through the settlement, it would be easier and faster with the kid. For no good reason, a ball started to knot in my gut.

Kel frowned. "The other adults wouldn't have let me poke around anyway." He headed back. "Come on."

The workshop was almost at the other end of the settlement and, walking inside, I could tell why. It was more of a junkyard than a proper working space.

I shook my head. How Eris had been able to find anything to use in all this scrap was beyond me. But she had been here this morning, I could taste it in the air.

I glanced around again, but saw no one. Other than the whirrs and whines of machinery, I heard nothing.

"Connor," the kid's voice wavered and the knot my gut tightened, ready for I didn't know what. "Can you come over here?"

The kid stood by a console of some kind, looked jury rigged together from what I could see. But it wasn't the comm or the scatter of parts that caught my attention.

It was the trail of blood staining the edge of the work bench.

My nostrils flared. Eris was injured, and someone was going to pay.

ERIS

*A*ll I could feel was cold.

Ice had worked its way around my fingers, knotted my hands and arms so tightly in its grip I couldn't even move.

Each breath stabbed thousands of icy daggers into my lungs.

I struggled to sit up, then the panic really began.

It wasn't just the ice that had frozen me, my arms were tied behind my back. A blindfold covered my eyes, and all I could hear was the wind whistling around me.

Had Connor with his injuries missed one of the bandits? Had there been someone else, hiding in the forest, waiting for revenge?

I tried to think back, but the sharp pain throbbing in my head made it hard to focus.

There was something about the pain that was important to remember...

Hyso.

Oh, Void.

"Hello?" I called out. "Can anyone hear me?"

No answer, just the wind in the trees, and then I could make out something else underneath the wind.

The low purr of an engine.

My cold, deadened senses finally put together the pieces. I was in the back of some sort of vehicle - from the snow I'd shaken off my face, obviously an uncovered one.

Thoughts stumbled through my head. Connor wouldn't even know where to find me. The loss terrified me as much as Hyso's attack.

My breath came in pants and gasps. "Put on your 'suit, Eris." I could almost hear him say the words. The mental exercise gave me enough space to gather my thoughts.

If I was in the back of something, and it was open, I should be able to get out, right?

I rolled and pushed myself until I sat up, my back resting against the edge of what felt like a low wall.

I stretched further, leaning out. Only empty space waited for me, no bars or wire cage over the bed of the vehicle. If Hyso could see me, well, there wasn't anything to be done for it.

Sitting up, I could feel the wind hit the side of my face. Not enough information to guess the speed of the vehicle, or the distance to the ground, but I could wait and wonder, or I could do something.

I shoved my legs together, and pushed backwards off the wall, biting my lips to stay silent in the desperate hope that whoever it was – Hyso? My mind still couldn't wrap around it, find a reason - somehow wouldn't notice I'd escaped, or, at least, not right away.

I tried to tuck my head as I fell, but for once I was grateful for the deep layers of snow. I didn't break anything on impact.

Now, to avoid freezing to death.

I rolled into a crouch, but just then the blindfold was ripped from my eyes.

I blinked in the sudden light.

Hyso stood before me, shaking his head. "You really are a major pain in the ass, do you know that?"

With more strength than I had suspected he possessed, he

heaved me over his shoulder and brought me back the few steps I'd managed to escape.

The vehicle, some sort of motorized sled fitted with runners, had two seats, one in front of the other. And a long, narrow open bed.

He tossed me back into the bed and this time fastened the rope around my arms to a loop of metal fixed in the sidewall, probably there to strap down wood, supplies, or whatever the sled was usually used for.

"You screwed up my ride out of here," he spat. "At least you could have the decency to stay put until I get you to somebody who actually wants you."

"Hyso, I have no idea what you're talking about," I stammered.

He whirled back towards me, his face contorted with rage. "Of course you don't. I had a perfectly reasonable setup going to get off this stupid planet. And then you and your boyfriend show up and screw everything up."

I tried to make sense of what he was saying. Finally, I came to a conclusion I couldn't stand to look at, but it was the only thing that made sense.

"Volsh? You were the one that told Volsh and his gang about the cyprtite?" Staggered, I leaned back, barely wincing as the metal loop dug into my spine. "What possible good could that have done?"

"It was an easy exchange. They get the rock, and when they came to pick it up, they'd give me a lift into some sort of civilization."

"But how did you even contact them? The magnetic storm..." I caught myself, struck by the obvious answer. "There is no storm, is there?"

"Everyone here is so stupid. All communications on and off planet come through systems I set up. It's easy to shut it down when I want, control what other people get from the outside."

He gestured wildly, and I cringed back as far as I could get from him. The snow fell faster, but he didn't seem to notice.

"I was hoping maybe to hook up with you, maybe get you to ditch that meathead, get a lift out with you, if you found a ride. But you weren't accommodating there, either."

My stomach flipped at the thought of him touching me, and I forced my face to stay neutral.

"Sure, we've got weird radiation patterns here, but a magnetic storm that lasted for almost a month? And people believed it." He rolled his eyes. "Everybody here believes each other, because we're all in each other's heads all the time."

That was weird, but he was on a roll. I had the feeling he'd been alone with his thoughts for so long all the bile was spilling out at once, and I was the lucky target.

"But I've got another offer for you-- so maybe you're not worthless after all."

I blinked. "An offer? What are you talking about?"

But he was done giving out information, apparently. He mounted the sled again in silence, and we started back up, wherever we were headed.

Facing the rear of the sled, I could only tell that the forest seemed to be getting thicker. Maybe we were heading uphill, maybe further into the mountains.

Who knew.

Cold and miserable, I slouched down out of the increasingly frigid wind.

Connor, come find me soon.

CONNOR

y head pounded, and the scent of Eris' blood threatened to tint my vision red. I fought down the rage. If I lost control, I wouldn't be any help to her.

When I found her, when she was safe… that would be another matter.

I didn't hear the kid call for help, but Waldar and Therra burst into the shop, Sion right behind them.

"Where. Is. Eris?" I growled, and the group took a step back.

Waldar stepped forward, face pale. "Son, we don't know. We just now heard from Kel she's missing. You know we'll help you look."

Silently, I pointed to the blood stain. "Where's the mech?"

Therra's face went blank for a moment, then she blinked. "I can't find him."

She looked at Sion and Waldar, as if for confirmation, but whatever it was seemed to have confused all three.

"He couldn't have," Sion breathed, then ran back out of the workshop.

I started after her, but Waldar rested a hand on my arm. "She'll be right back, I promise. Just checking on something."

Kel stood by the console, fingers dancing over the keyboard. "Hyso has this locked down." He gnawed his lower lip. "Really tight."

I could smell the worry coming off Waldar.

"I take it that's not normal procedure."

Waldar shook his head. "I can't imagine why it would be encrypted. These are systems that run the whole communications for the settlement. Why would Hyso do that?"

"And why didn't we know?" Therra muttered. Both Waldar and Therra were obviously concerned.

"There's something you need to understand," Therra started.

"Unless it's about how I'm going to get Eris back, I'm not sure I need to know."

"I can get into this," Kel brought us back to the matter at hand.

"You sure, kid?"

"Yeah."

He glanced at the other adults, who looked surprised.

"Hyso is a jerk. And Eris is really nice," he continued in a much softer voice. "She's really good about answering questions and stuff, not just telling me to shut up."

"Do it then."

Long minutes stretched while the kid did something, lots of somethings, that made me glad I wasn't a tech monkey.

"Are you still--"

He shut me down. "It'll go easier if you're not over my shoulder."

The kid was right. I wanted him to do the job, I needed to trust him. Nothing I knew about what he was doing, anyway.

I turned to Therra and Waldar. "So, while we've got time, you tell me whatever you were going to before. If you think it's relevant. Otherwise, I'd rather have your thoughts on where he might've taken Eris and why."

Waldar leaned on the edge of one of the workbenches. "You're right, let's start with the basics and then move out. That's the better way to run a hunt."

"Why he would've taken Eris, I can't possibly imagine. And that's something else that concerns me, but we'll get to that in a minute."

"Where," he ran his hands through his gray hair. "There's nowhere to go. This is the only settlement on the planet. Other than the shallow caves we've used as shelters for sudden snow-storms when on patrol, there's nothing out there."

"Could he be headed to one of the caves?"

Therra snorted. "Hyso has never been interested in hunting, or going out on patrol. I doubt if he'd even know where to find them."

Waldar frowned. "He could, if he was able to get through somebody's shields who didn't notice..." he trailed off.

"What are you talking about?" I snapped. My headache hadn't been helped by any of their round-about explanations, and I didn't see how any of this was getting me closer to a location for Eris.

Waldar leaned back, braced himself on his hands. "I might have enough of a mechanical background to have helped on the ship when we came over, but I'm not a scientist or a doctor."

"Didn't figure you for one, so go on."

"Sion is as trained up as she can be out here, but she doesn't have an answer, either. All we know is that, not long after we landed here, all of us started to get thoughts, flashes of each other's minds."

Therra broke in. "Sion thinks it has something to do with the planet's magnetic field. It reverses more often than usual, it seems, hell on a lot of navigational instruments."

Waldar picked up the thread again. "Anyhow, I don't under-stand it, all I know is that it got stronger in the next generation and the one after. Enough that we were worried that if the secret got out, someone would come and take our kids away for study, or worse."

I stared at him blankly. "You're telling me that something on this planet has caused everyone in the colony to become telepathic?" I looked between the two of them. "Have I got that right?"

I thought of what Doc would do with this, a world that altered brain patterns. She'd been interested in all sorts of mutations, engineered and natural. Void knew she'd tried to cram enough of them into us. The settlement had been right to worry.

Waldar looked abashed, but Therra raised her chin. "What does it matter? We don't get a lot of visitors other than the Imperial agents. No one needed to know."

"You do know the Empire has telepaths of its own? They often use them in negotiations."

Therra rolled her eyes. "We had figured that out. On one of our last trading expeditions off-planet, we made some acquisitions, bought some disguises, if you will."

"How do you disguise telepathy?", I growled. "Other than just lying about it."

"We weren't lying, it wasn't any of your business. Besides, we're not the only ones with secrets."

Sion came back in, her face gray, carrying a slim gray box. "One set missing, and," she blurted out, "I don't know when he took them."

Waldar shoved some junk off the workbench and she laid the long rectangular box on it.

The box unlocked when she placed her thumb in a recessed slot. The cover slid open to reveal two long rows of paired silver discs.

"Neural blockers?" I wondered.

Waldar nodded. "Everyone that comes anywhere near the Imperials wears a pair while they're here. It's odd, wearing them now. Kind of like having an itch you can't scratch."

Sion ran her finger down the row, pointed to an empty slot where a pair was missing.

"They block whatever it is," she waved, "we've developed since coming here. We've tested them, felt we needed to." Sion closed the box, and her eyes, as if looking at charts I couldn't see.

"Even if, with a probe of someone wearing the blockers, there's not a response, it just feels like someone with a low-grade shield, maybe something that could be developed through meditation or any one of a number of mental exercises. But it also keeps the ability from being used."

Therra glowered at the box. "I hate wearing them. It's like being suddenly blind or deaf, something that I'm used to having all the time, not even thinking about it until it's gone."

Sion shook her head. "I don't know how long this pair has been missing. No one is supposed to have access to them but me or Petro."

Waldar patted her hand. "You're not to blame."

"You don't understand. If Hyso has been wearing them nonstop for days or even weeks..." she shrugged. "The younger generation especially is very acclimated, even possibly dependent on the new sense. I think it could unbalance him."

"More importantly," Waldar added. "It would explain why we had no idea of anything he's been planning or doing."

"I'd say that was an understatement," Kel added. "I'm into his computer. It's not like he kept a diary or anything, but I can put together a good bit just from his logs."

"Let me see that." As I stepped to the console, I put a hand on his shoulder. "Good job."

"I'm scared for Eris," he whispered.

"So am I," I muttered, my eyes flicking over the hundreds of transmissions altered, apparently sent without the colony's knowledge.

"For a group of telepaths, it's a little surprising to realize you have a traitor in your midst." Maybe that wasn't fair, but I'd apologize later. Maybe.

"This is what I'm worried about the most." Kel flicked to a set of transmissions date stamped early this morning.

"Messages between an unknown sender, and Hyso. They're talking about taking a passenger to a valley to the north of here, and then Hyso getting a payment." His fingers tapped on the side of the screen nervously. "The weirder thing is, I don't recognize what channel it came in on, I've never seen traffic on it before."

I looked at the channel and my blood turned to ice. "I have. Get me the coordinates they're talking about, now."

Kel flicked open a map, pulled and enlarged the display until a valley to the north of the settlement was clear. "That's where they say, but-"

Waldar pushed forward. "Idiot. That's in the middle of chirl territory. There's never a good reason to go there."

"Maybe, or maybe not." I tapped the screen, remembering the fight with the white monkey things that had attacked Waldar when we were on patrol. "If something had taken over their valley, would that explain why the troop of them had come so close to the settlement?"

Waldar rubbed the side of his head. "Only if that ship held something bigger and meaner. Not much of that around here."

"Oh," I thought about the attack on the *Daedalus*, about the ship that had shot down the *Nyx*. "I wouldn't be surprised."

"If that's where they're going, they'd almost be there by now," Therra said. "I'm guessing he's got a lead on us by a couple of hours, at least."

She looked at me inquiringly and I nodded. I couldn't be sure when Hyso snatched her, but that fit with when Eris had woken up and the scent of the blood trail.

"It'd be fastest to take the bandit ship," Waldar said. "Except that none of us can pilot it."

"I probably could, not well, but I could manage," I admitted.

"But we'd lose any chance of surprise. I don't think Hyso would expect we'd break his encryption. And we're going to need every advantage we can get."

"Dad, what about the sleds?" Therra asked.

"That should work," Waldar answered. "I tinkered a bit with two of the cargo runners. They're a good bit faster than originally built. Birthday present for my girl a few years back."

I started planning. "What's the range on this talent? At what point will Hyso know that we're coming, 'sense' us?"

Therra shook her head. "If he's still wearing the blocker, it works both ways. He won't 'see' us, we won't 'see' him."

It was an 'if' I didn't like, but one I might have to live with. I headed towards the workshop door, more than ready to get going.

"Fine, but you keep your feelers or whatever out. The instant you think he might be in range and without the blockers, let me know." A thought struck. "Can you sense when we're getting close to Eris?"

"Maybe. Usually we don't pick up on strangers' thoughts very well. A general idea of their intentions maybe, but nothing clearer."

Intentions? "Then how could Volsh kidnap Aggie without anyone figuring it out?"

All three of the adults stopped cold.

"Bastard!" Therra yelled, and kicked over a workbench, scattering the piles of scrap and tools to the floor with a clatter. "I'd bet my last credit Hyso was in it with them. Warned them to be prepared."

Sion nodded. "Neural blockers aren't impossible to find, obviously. For a heist of that magnitude, it would've been a reasonable investment."

"Calm down, girl," Waldar admonished his daughter. "Doesn't change anything about our current hunt."

No. But the knot in my gut only tightened at the idea of Eris being held by someone who would risk a kid like that.

"Fine, let's get moving," was all I said.

"We could use another hand," Waldar said as we left the work-shop. "Each runner can carry two pretty easily without losing speed."

"Raz would be a good choice," I answered. "She did well yesterday."

"What about me?" Kel cried out.

"Not a chance, kid. If you want to help, you take apart that comm and anything else that bastard touched. What other secrets has he been hiding? I want to know it all."

He scowled, but headed back inside. "You'd better get her back," he called over his shoulder as the doors slammed behind him.

Whatever else was out there, waiting in the snow, there was no question about that.

ERIS

When I woke, my muscles were still stiff and cramped from the cold. A dim, pale green light illuminated the small room I was in. I blinked, tried to refocus, and looked around again. Some sort of a small cargo hold, not much more than a storage closet, really.

I flexed my fingers behind my back and swore at the pins and needles racing up and down my arms. It was better than the numbness in my feet. Maybe. Another wave of tiny stabs had me reconsidering that opinion.

Nothing else was in the hold, other than a stack of matte black crates. Three of them lined the wall across from me, with a column four high stacked on top.

Sharp spasms replaced the numbness in my legs. I tried to stretch them out, but the stack of crates was in the way.

I closed my eyes, took a deep breath.

Horrible to say, but at least I was back inside. I didn't have to worry about a full-fledged panic attack striking on top of everything else.

First things first. Honestly, I had no idea what that should be, but being able to stand was high on my list.

I kicked my legs back and forth, trying to speed up the flow of blood.

My foot bumped the corner of one of the crates, and the topmost one teetered, as if the stack hadn't been placed very securely.

I stopped moving, curled back into a ball. The last thing I wanted was to draw attention to the fact I was awake.

Or did I? I'd already been kidnapped by a mad mechanic and driven halfway around a frozen planet in a snowstorm. If they were going to kill me, whoever they were, they would have done it when the popsicle delivery guy had dropped me off.

I inched closer to the crates and started kicking, watching the top most in the stack slowly become more and more unbalanced

One. More...

With a crash and clatter, three of the stacked crates tumbled to the deck floor. I managed to turn my face away in time, as what looked like a random collection of scrap metal and wires hit the floor and bounced everywhere.

Once the chaos died down, I waited. Surely, if anyone was around, they'd have heard that commotion.

But no one came.

I twisted around until my fingers brushed against a sharp piece of metal. There wasn't a good way to get a grip on it without hurting myself.

Finally, I managed to blindly jam the shard firmly between two crates at the bottom of the stack. Pivoting until my bound wrists could reach the edge, I slowly, carefully, began the tedious process of sawing myself free.

I'd mentally gone through the first four steps in cycle flushing a scoop engine when the chords weakened enough that I could wiggle them the rest of the way loose.

My hands still looked a little blue tinged, and the red marks around my wrists weren't going to fade anytime soon, but I was free, and that was the important part.

A sharp bit of metal wasn't much of a weapon, but, with the hem of my shirt wrapped around a corner of the long irregular triangle, it would be better than nothing.

Gingerly, I pulled it back out from between the crates, trying to find a way to hold it so that I would cut my shirt and not myself.

Then I saw it.

In the center of the rough triangle, an ornate X was etched, the swoops and curls running off the edges of the piece of metal.

I ran my finger over the shape, but there was no question. I knew that X, as well as I had known the other letters that I'd drawn out so carefully to decorate my ship's hull.

I looked around again at the scattered pieces of metal around me with new eyes. It was all wreckage of the *Nyx*.

Somehow, this was all that was left of my ship. The horror of the last few days came crashing down. Beyond anything, I wanted to curl up, and cry until I was numb.

My fingers fisted around the scrap of hull and the sharp well of blood brought my situation back to me.

I'd been lucky no one came. I couldn't keep counting on that.

Shoving away my sorrow, I sliced the edge of shirt to wrap around my makeshift dagger as planned, and moved to the door.

I looked back at the scrap that had been so much of my life when a flash caught my eye. A cube, not much bigger than my two fists. Blue lights faintly glimmered through the dark silver panels.

"Nixie?" I whispered, tearing through the rest of the crates, looking for components.

Why had someone bothered to collect all this rubbish and refuse from the wreck?

The question circled in my mind but I batted it to the side.

It didn't matter right now.

Nixie's core sat in my lap, and there were enough bits and pieces around to build an input mechanism.

Terribly primitive, but it would do the job. I finished and

fastened it against her side. It was ugly, and I wouldn't tell her what it looked like. But it was the best I'd be able to do until I had more parts.

Head aching, I rubbed my temples, reaching for a memory - something that had been no more than a game. An ancient tapping code we'd amused each other with during the long days between jobs.

All right, I struggled to learn it, Nixie, of course, had absorbed it in a flash.

nixie are you there

Her lights flashed and I had to tap frantically for her to slow down. When I could read her message, the tears threatened again.

eris losing power glad you came goodbye

The hell with that.

Now that I'd found her again, goodbye wasn't an option.

I was on a ship again. I could do anything.

hang on getting us out hang on

The door wasn't even locked. Whoever it was was confident that I'd stay where I was put. Their mistake.

A short corridor led straight to the cockpit. This looked like a craft for a single person, sleek and small, but with even less space than I'd had on the *Nyx*. The cockpit design wasn't like anything I'd ever seen, but right now I didn't need to figure out how to fly it, just borrow a little juice.

are you charging

Yes and looking around

I sagged against the console in relief. Of course she was.

Nixie's charging cycle gave me time to think. The only reason I could imagine for the collection of the wreckage of the *Nyx* was if someone wanted to see if anyone was aboard when she went down. Which meant the pilot of this ship was whoever Connor had been so worried about.

That wasn't good.

While I was thinking, I pulled apart a speaker from the other console, started working, stripping wires.

"Nixie, this is a test. While you're in there, see if you can figure a way to ground this ship."

will do, she blinked in answer.

The cockpit was completely shielded, I couldn't even see where we were. While Nixie finished charging, I took a chance, raised enough of the systems to take a look outside.

Snow. And trees. No big surprises there. At least it appeared I was still on Skarth 5.

Ice water ran through my veins. I hadn't even thought about it before. I could have been taken elsewhere, and, while I really wanted to get off this ball of ice, I'd never find my way back to Connor.

And somehow that mattered, mattered just as much as finding Nixie had.

I kept flicking sensors off and on, triggering the ship's cameras in sequence around the perimeter for as short bursts as possible, hoping to continue avoiding detection, but desperately needing any more information. The ship lay nestled in a narrow valley, with dense groves of trees on the steep slopes.

There.

On the port side of the ship, Hyso stood facing a tall figure in a black uniform. Something about it looked...wrong.

I zoomed the camera in, trying to get a look at the man's face, but he wore a black domed helmet, completely opaque.

Apparently, somebody's issues were worse than mine. Good to know.

Nixie flashed green.

"Ready to go?" I asked.

I have all sorts of things to tell you, she flashed.

I decoupled her from the console and made my way back towards the room I'd been held in.

On the wall to the side of the door I started searching. "It's got to be here somewhere," I muttered.

The door slid open and Nixie flashed *you're welcome.*

Show off. The half ladder lowered me down what the schematics had shown as an emergency hatch under the belly of the ship.

Once I was on the ground, I hurried towards the starboard landing strut, tucking myself behind it.

And waited, listening.

I could hear Hyso ranting from here, every word as clear as when I was in the back of the sled.

Apparently, his new friend hadn't calmed him down any.

"You owe me," Hyso screamed. "I did what you asked for and you owe me. You have to take me, I can't go back now."

Whatever the black-suited stranger said just sent Hyso into more of a tailspin.

"You said you wanted all survivors of the crash. I brought her."

A pause and Hyso's shoulders deflated a little.

"Fine, yes, there were two of them. But the other one, he's a big guy. There's no way in hell I'd be able to get him."

He kicked the snow, looking like a scolded kid. "Seriously? You want him that bad, just wait. He doesn't look too bright, but eventually he'll figure out she's gone, come looking for her. Scout around, I'm sure you'll find him out of the settlement and alone."

Hyso snorted. Every creepy feeling I ever had about him was never more justified than in that moment. He glared at the ship, and I pressed myself tighter against the strut.

"Guy seems kind of like an idiot to me, but who knows what women want."

Whatever we want is certainly nothing like you, I thought.

Nixie's cube grew hot in my hand.

"Just a second, Nixie," I whispered. "I need Hyso to turn away."

The black-suited man took a step forwards, then another, his movements awkward, inhuman.

Hyso's voice grew shrill. "I did what you wanted. I did what you wanted and you owe me now."

But he didn't wait for an answer this time, merely spun and ran the best he could through the deep snow away from the stranger.

It wasn't much of a chase. With two great bounds, the black-clad figure was on Hyso's back. A sickening snap echoed through the narrow valley, and Hyso's body lay limp.

Now would be a good time for me to go, I tried to tell my legs. While the completely terrifying man is distracted by the possibly less terrifying but still crazy corpse of the man who kidnapped me.

Come on, body. But it wasn't until I glanced down at Nixie that the paralysis released me.

Run Eris run. As far from the ship as possible. Run run run run run.
I ran.

CONNOR

I could see the valley ahead, a thin crack in the mountains. Didn't need a map to tell me that's where we were going. Every atom of my body drew me to it.

The sleds sped silently through the snow, faster than I would have expected due to Waldar's modifications, but something in my chest howled in frustration.

I rode behind Therra, with Waldar and Raz's sled close behind us.

For most of the past hour, we'd hunched over the sleek machine in silence, anger and urgency driving us on.

Therra turned her head slightly so I could hear her words over the howling wind. "So, you and that skittish woman, really? Doesn't look like much of a fighter."

If it hadn't been for my worry, I might've smiled. Even in the midst of chaos, Therra was nothing but direct in going after her target.

"Really," I replied.

She shrugged as she darted around a tree branch, somehow getting even more speed out of the sled.

"Dad said you guys were mated, that I couldn't keep you.

Seems like an odd match to me, but I guess you know what you want."

I nodded. What I wanted, what I needed, was to have Eris safe beside me. Back in the cabin, up in the ship, anywhere.

A flash of terror struck me, and a vision of running across a snow field passed before my eyes. Before I could make sense of it, my ears picked up a low rumble.

"Go to the side," I yelled, and wildly gestured for Waldar to follow us, away from the path we'd been hollowing.

"What?"

"Just do it!"

She sheared off, shot sharply to the side, just in time for a wall of snow to come thundering out of the valley.

Even with the increased speed, the wall of white that came crashing down from the valley clipped the end of the sled, sending it spinning through the trees and tossing us off its back.

As we flew off, I snagged the back of Therra's jacket with one hand, clawing for purchase on the trees and branches we crashed into.

"Breath in, and hold it!" I shouted. And then followed my own advice.

In seconds, the wall of white had gone past us, rumbling below, then all was still.

Taking stock, the snow was only up to my shoulder, and that last expansion of my chest had given me plenty of room to breathe.

"Hold on," and, with a wrench, I threw Therra up out of the snowpack to the surface, and then climbed up the rest of the tree to follow her.

She looked around wildly. "Dad, did you see where dad's sled went?"

I had to get to Eris. If she was caught in this, every minute would count.

But I couldn't abandon the people who had ridden up here into danger to save her.

Therra called out for her father and Raz frantically, wading in circles.

"Quiet," I muttered. I listened, then smelled hot metal. Either our sled or Waldar's. It was a start.

"Stay there." I moved from tree to tree, no longer worried what anyone saw, guessed about my engineering, my design.

There'd been far too many secrets already.

I dropped down over the scent, started digging, pulling up huge handfuls of snow. Before I hit the sled, I found Raz. Her face was pale and strained, and she yelped when I lifted her from the snow, but otherwise she seemed unharmed.

Therra was right behind me. "Is my father there?" she gasped.

Raz nodded. "He got trapped under the sled, we weren't fast enough to make it out. But I heard him," her eyes fixed on Therra's. "I heard him just a minute ago. I think he's fine."

"Get behind those trees." I saw argument in Therra's face, and cut it off. "Do it, I don't have time."

The two women took shelter behind the thick trunk of a tree up slope while I worked to dig a tunnel around the lower edge of the sled.

It wouldn't have been impossible to pick the whole thing up and lift it out of the way - if there had been anything more solid to stand on. As it was, the harder I strained to lift it, the deeper I'd sink in myself. Wouldn't do anyone any good.

But the angle of the sled and the slope of the hill could work for me.

I dug fast and furiously, refusing to think about Eris until this job was done.

"You still there, Raz?" A faint voice emerged from the snow.

"She's safe," I answered for her. "And so's Therra. I'll have you out in a minute."

"I'm fine," he coughed. "Go get your wife."

"Therra would kill us all, you know that, right?"

"Knew I raised that girl right…" His voice trailed off as I dug the last trench, then half walked, half swam in the snow uphill for whatever leverage I could get.

"Hang on," I called out and then kicked at the sled with all my strength.

With a groan of metal, it teetered, then rolled away, exposing Waldar's prone form. Therra and Raz rushed over, and pulled Waldar up to a sitting position.

"Go now," he commanded. "We'll be fine." He tapped the side of his head. "Help's on the way."

I nodded and was off, racing to the valley over the hardening snow pack.

When I arrived, it was easy to see what had triggered the avalanche.

Wreckage was strewn everywhere, scattered across the valley floor, twisted metal up in the trees. Enough of it survived to recognize a Hunter's Dart - likely one of the ones that attacked the *Daedalus* and blew the *Nyx* out of the sky.

Eris couldn't have survived if she'd been on board. Numbness crept through me. I'd kill them all. Track them, destroy every last Hunter, grind them into the dust until no one remembered their name.

Because nothing else was left.

A roar broke through me, echoing from the valley walls, taunting me with my own pain and rage.

Connor?

I spun, but couldn't see her. "Eris! Where are you?"

Get me, please. I'm so cold.

I sprinted to a stand of trees half-way up the opposite side of the valley. "Eris?" I called. *Eris?*

I'm here. Nixie told me to run, but I didn't get far enough.

"Tell me when I'm close, I'm getting you out."

I knew you'd come.

I could sense her, almost see her in my mind, wedged between three thick trunks. Hard packed snow kept her upright, but, between the lack of oxygen and the cold, she was losing the battle to stay awake.

"I'm almost there, honey." The next swipe at the snow uncovered a dark curl of hair, and I slowed my pace. "Working you out now."

In moments, I held her pressed to my chest, trying to force warmth back into her.

Her eyes flickered open, and, despite the freezing cold and the wreckage around us, it was a perfect day.

"I thought I was losing my mind," she whispered. "I could hear you in my head."

"Me, too," I pulled her the rest of the way to her feet, keeping one arm around her shoulders. "Believe it or not, there's a semi-reasonable explanation for that. It can wait until we're back to the settlement, though."

Eris leaned into me. "I don't think I can walk that far." When she looked up, smiling, I knew she'd be fine. We'd be fine. "Just so you know, I'm going to argue about you carrying me."

"Humor me for a bit." I swung her into my arms and relaxed as her head nestled onto my shoulder. A random thought struck me. "Did you say something about Nixie?"

Eris patted her jacket front, which I noticed stuck out in an odd shape. "Found her. She knew the ship was going to blow. I'll ask her about it later when I get her hooked back to proper comms. She flashes too fast."

None of that made a bit of sense, and I didn't care. "When we get back, I'll have Waldar show us a new recipe for dinner."

"Maybe breakfast," she answered sleepily. "For dinner, I just want-"

Whatever she wanted was lost when a black streak knocked into my back.

I rolled, tucking my body around Eris, but another blow struck her from my arms.

Spinning, I faced my opponent, half-knowing what I'd find before I turned.

The Hunter had survived.

ERIS

$\mathcal{T}$he black-suited thing that killed Hyso faced Connor.

"Eris, get away." Connor yelled.

Like hell, I thought.

Frantically searching, I couldn't see anything that would help. Snow and trees and more trees and snow. Except, in the tree line, something glinted in the weak sun.

I moved towards it, slowly. Connor strode across the white valley floor as confidentially as I would have moved down the deck of a ship. But I could feel the snow shift and settle beneath my feet.

If I fell now, he'd be distracted. And the thing he faced was worse than the pack of yorgs that had nearly killed us before.

They fought in silence, only grunts and the impact of flesh where they struck at each other. I risked a glance, biting my lips so that I didn't call out.

Connor and the thing moved almost too fast to see, crossing the snow, in and out of trees. I could only catch glimpses of their battle when they grappled, straining against each other.

Then Connor flipped, somehow got behind the Hunter, with

his arms wrapped around its neck. He squeezed and, no matter how the things thrashed, it couldn't break free.

Finally, it spoke, its voice grating, somehow more artificial than even Nixie's.

"All results of the *Daedalus* experiment are to be returned to Base."

"Try it," Connor snarled, hate and fury flowing off him.

The meaning of the thing's words hit me. "All results of the *Daedalus* experiment." It meant Connor and his brothers.

Not a chance.

I grabbed a long shard of the ship's hull that had embedded itself in the tree and turned back to where they fought. I might not be able to do much, but, if Connor had a weapon, he could crack that thing's helmet, look it in the eye.

But, as I approached, the Hunter went limp, then, in a flash, twisted, throwing Connor over its shoulder into the snow before it.

Connor rolled, pulling the Hunter with him, and the two flipped over each other until their momentum drove the pair into a stand of trees, the impact splitting the combatants apart.

The Hunter recovered first, staggering to its feet slowly, implacably.

"Wake up!" I shouted, but Conner didn't move. A fine spray of red dotted the snow, and I my breath caught in my chest.

The Hunter took another step towards Connor.

"Keep away from him, you bastard!"

It gave no sign it even registered my presence, and, suddenly, fury outweighed any fear.

"This is all your fault!" I threw the metal at its helmet, which did nothing, except make me angrier. "You destroyed my ship! And got me kidnapped!" I spun, looking for something else to throw, and found a rock sticking up from the snow by a tree trunk.

The rock hit the helmet with a satisfying thunk. There must

have been just enough weight, just enough of a sharp edge on the rock, that a fine crack appeared.

The Hunter stopped its advance on Connor. A not-small tinge of fear mixed with the thrill of my small victory.

But I was tired of being afraid. I was well and truly angry now, so I found another rock.

"And, worst of all," I flung it, missing the helmet but smacking the Hunter's shoulder, "you got me stuck on a damn planet!"

Maybe that last rock wasn't such a hot idea. The tree trunk at my back kept me from retreating further, but I was tired of running.

The Hunter slowly pivoted its torso until it faced me. "Hazards to the mission must be eliminated."

And, apparently, I'd been elevated to the level of hazard. Good.

I scrambled for another rock, but found nothing but snow. The first snowball splattered on the Hunter's uniform, but didn't slow its progress. I flung snow frantically, hoping to uncover another piece of wreckage, another rock, anything.

The Hunter's implacable steps neither slowed nor veered in their course. Straight at me.

My fingers wrapped around something hard and thin. Another piece of the Hunter's ship, a jagged section of strut, from the feel of it.

The Hunter kept advancing, but I waited, thinking. Hand-thrown missiles just didn't have enough impact. The worst I'd done was annoy it, crack its helmet.

Without any other weapon, my best chance would be to try to widen that crack. But I couldn't trust my aim. I'd have to wait until the Hunter was almost on me.

One step, then another.

My throat dried, almost too tight to swallow.

The black helmet only showed my reflection, hair everywhere, eyes huge and lips thin with terror. Like a greased spring, the

Hunter leapt forwards. I barely had time to raise my makeshift dagger to strike at the cracked helmet.

It struck it out of my hand, and it spun lazily into the snow.

Before I could twist out of the way, the Hunter grabbed my shoulders, shaking me so hard my head spun. A roar echoed in my ears, and suddenly the Hunter was gone, and I fell into the snow.

I staggered back to my feet. Connor plowed the Hunter to the side, then lifted it over his head, and flung it away with a sickening crunch.

The Hunter lay impaled, twitching on a jagged tree stump, sparks arcing around the hole in its chest.

I ran to Connor's side, and we watched it struggle against gravity, and sink lower, its limbs slowly going limp. "All results...."

Then the black-clad form was silent.

It was over.

Connor sagged a little, and I wrapped my arms around him, listening to his heart beat.

Are you-? Is it-?

Our words and thoughts spilled over each other, and I stopped, hands pressed over my mouth. "That's going to take some getting used to."

Connor pulled me back into his embrace. "Can't be any harder than the last week."

When the others came over the ridge, they found us laughing helplessly, tangled together in the snow.

CONNOR

*I*n the back of the large, all-terrain vehicle Neva had sent for us, Sion checked us over while Eris filled us in on the missing pieces of Hyso's plan.

Waldar shook his head. "I'll go back up, get his body tomorrow before the yorgs or chirls get it. He may have been a bastard, but he was our bastard. Can't help but feel like we let him down somehow."

Eris pushed her hair out of her eyes, winced at the lump on her head. "I don't think so. I think he was just one of those people who wanted more and nothing was ever going to be enough. But I guess we'll never know."

Therra leaned back, eyes closed. "If he wanted to leave that badly, he just should have said so. He wouldn't have been that hard to replace." She nudged her father's boot with her own. "Unlike some others."

The color rose high in Eris' cheeks. "I'm really sorry about that." She drew a medium sized silver cube from her jacket. "I forget that Nixie sometimes doesn't think about human consequences."

I was afraid to ask, but... "What, exactly, did you and Nixie do?"

"I wanted her to ground the ship. I was terrified he'd lift, take me somewhere, anywhere," she whispered. "I think she triggered a self-destruct routine."

A pit opened in my stomach, and I pulled her towards me, buried my face in her hair. "Just would have taken longer to find you, that's all."

"Huh," was Therra's only comment. "Maybe there's more to you than I thought. Good job."

By the time we reached the settlement, Sion had checked us both over. She shook her head over my already closing injuries.

"Wish all my patients healed up as fast as you."

It felt good not to have a secret to hide.

At the cabin, I steered Eris towards the shower, to finish getting her thawed out, but she headed to the kitchen, peeling off her jacket as she walked.

"Hungry?"

"Starving, but I think there's a power port in here I can use to get Nixie back online." She puttered with the silver cube for a minute, then turned back, leaning against the counter.

I couldn't help but smile at her focus, "Glad you got her back."

"One issue solved," Eris started a loose braid of her hair, fingers nervously dancing.

But what do we do about this?

I kneaded her shoulders, pulled her close. "We can ask Sion. They've got to have devised ways to not have everyone in town in everyone else's thoughts all the time. Besides, I haven't heard anyone else in my head, have you?"

She shook her head slowly, clearly thinking something over in that clever mind. "If it's just between us, I want to run a few experiments."

"Really," I snorted, then caught my breath as she ran her hand over her own breast. The unfamiliar sensation spiraled through me, kicking off my own wave of want and need for her.

"Oh, really," she answered, leaning into me, and, the sweetness of her mouth, the twining of our tongues as they slipped together, dragged us both under the feedback of sensation.

When we surfaced, I pulled away, fought to clear my head. "So," I stopped, almost afraid of her answer more than I was fighting the Hunter. But this was another question that had to be faced.

"What do we do from here?"

"Well," she turned back, ran a finger over Nixie's side. "I guess it depends."

Depends. Not what I wanted to hear. I felt as if I were hunting over thin ice, senses deadened, unable to tell where it might crack beneath me.

"I think we make a pretty good team, don't you?"

"Definitely," I answered, running my fingers through her hair, careful of the hit she'd taken.

"And I'm pretty sure that the settlement would sell us Volsh's ship. It hasn't been maintained, but there's some good lines there."

"You said 'us'."

"Well," she looked up, eyes blazing with humor. "We are married, after all."

I laughed and swung her into my arms, kissing her deeply. "I guess we are, at that."

"As for where we should go after here? You remember how Nixie took a peek in the *Daedalus'* files," she trailed off.

I frowned as a terrible thought struck me. "When you were on the Hunter's Dart, you didn't...."

"Just enough for her to power up of bit. You wouldn't believe how quickly cold drains her. And, she might have done a little looking around there, too."

"Of course she did." I gave up. A mischievous AI had access to dangerous and classified information that could get us killed - or give us the clues to find out what happened to the *Daedalus*. What could go wrong?

But that's for tomorrow, Eris answered the whirl of my thoughts.

Tonight... and I couldn't tell who thought it, or who answered.

And it didn't matter in the least.

EPILOGUE

I "felt" Connor coming into the ship, long before I heard him.

In the bridge, getting Nixie settled, I 'called'.

The new voice had started to feel comfortable. We never did start picking up on any thoughts of the rest of the settlement, and that was fine with me. One extra person in my head was quite enough.

In the week since the incident with the Hunter, we'd learned more than a few tips for keeping our privacy - and for only opening ourselves up to physical feedback when we wanted it.

I grinned as I slid out from under the console, letting my eyes range over Connor's lean body as he entered the bridge.

Maybe "wanted" was too weak of a word.

Desired. That was closer.

Connor shot back a cocky smile and an image that made me shiver, but kept to the point at hand.

"What do you think, Nixie," he asked, "any luck with the old AI?"

If she could have, she would have sniffed. "*That barely competent program scarcely qualifies as an AI. Artificial, certainly. However, he'll*

ELIN WYN

be useful for some of the routine work while I'm correlating the information from the Hunter's ship with that from the Daedalus."

Volsh's ship - our ship now, I corrected myself - hadn't taken much to get up and running once I'd undone the damage from my trap. A few new parts and she'd be faster than the *Nyx* I realized, with a tinge of betrayal.

Kel had turned into a promising assistant, and his new role as the settlement's lead mech had softened the blow when both Sion and I had forbidden him to come with us.

"Have you decided on a new name?" Connor asked, trailing his hands over the panels.

I'd thought about it, the chaos that had brought us together. The path that we'd chosen to follow.

"*Seeker,*" I answered.

He smiled and pulled me to my feet, into his embrace. We stared out the forward screens, as if already on our way.

"Do you think your brothers are looking, too?"

"I know they are."

"Then we'll find them, or they'll find us."

He nodded, "Somewhere, out in the Fringe, we'll all find the answers. But for now, I have what I'm looking for."

And so do I.

THE END

LETTER FROM ELIN

Dear Reader,

Another brother found, clues to what happened on the Daedalus, and a few more pieces to the puzzle...

I have to admit, as much fun as it was to write Eris and Connor's story, Nixie is a blast to write!

In the next book, Imperial spy Zayda has to decide who to trust when she's betrayed and sent to a satellite prison. Certainly not the hulking mystery man with no memory who lands at her feet, right? Of course not... ;p

You'll love Caged, because things are just getting hotter.

No Past. No Trust. No Way Out.

Click here to read *Caged*.

XOXO,

Elin

PREVIEW OF CAGED: STAR BREED
BOOK THREE

Chapter One: Zayda

Red, green, blue. Red, green, blue. The tags for the meds in the inventory flowed by in a sea of color, the only bright spots in the grey, dingy clinic.

Red, green, blue.

I'd done this yesterday, would do it again tomorrow since it counted as a useful task for the station.

"Take a break, Zayda," Denon called from the other corner of the prison clinic. "You're always working too hard."

Nominally assigned as the clinic medic, Denon didn't seem to worry at all about staying busy and useful. I glanced at my cuff. Still bright steady green. Good.

Maybe the time we spent patching up idiots who got into fights, or growers who ended up on the wrong end of equipment earned him enough points to coast through.

I'd only been here for two weeks. Not long enough to have it figured out. I was waiting for a sign, some indication of which way to jump.

But nothing yet.

Red, green, blue.

"Come on, Zayda." Denon had sidled up next to me. I hadn't noticed his approach. Being trapped here was getting to me, wearing down my sharp edges.

His arm rested around my waist, making my skin crawl, but I kept a careful smile on my face. Until I knew who to trust and how I was getting out of here, I couldn't stand to lose the clinic as a safe place.

Training made it easier to put up with a lot. But even I have limits.

I started to make another excuse, but was saved by the opening of the clinic doors. Jado and Malik, hauling a third man between them.

As co-captains of the Skulls, the satellite's largest gang, they had sent plenty of people to the clinic, sometimes their own members.

But then I got a better look at the man they brought in with them.

Jado and Malik were big. This guy was bigger, even slumped unconscious, his arms stretched over their shoulders, legs and feet pulling behind as they dragged him through the door.

"Cuffs told us to bring this dude in," Jado said. "Too messed up to even get off the shuttle on his own power."

I raised an eyebrow. The shuttle that brought prisoners up to the satellite was programmed to stop recycling air as soon as the airlock doors opened.

Prisoners had two minutes to disembark. Occasionally someone would insist on trying to stay aboard for the return trip back to the station.

It never ended well.

By the end of that two minutes they were usually convinced to try their chances on the satellite.

Denon rolled his eyes. "Put him on one of the cots until he comes out of it. Doesn't look like he's bleeding. Not much for me to do."

I slid out from under his arm. "I'll do a quick scan on him, just in case."

Denon shrugged and I tapped my cuff. "May as well keep the meter filled."

From across the room the guy was big. Standing next to his cot, he was massive. Muscles bulged from his arms and chest, his shoulders too wide to be fully supported by the narrow cot.

There was no way he would fit into our antiquated full body scanner, and I didn't even know if it was running today. I grabbed one of the handhelds and started at his feet.

The readings for - Oh. That was interesting.

I kept my eyes on the scanner and my mouth shut. But my mind spun frantically.

Jado and Malik were bullshitting with Denon. No one paid attention, no one cared.

In a career working for the Imperial spymaster you hear a lot of rumors. The vast majority are lies, speculation, or on a good day somebody's drug filled hallucinations laid on top of something they just watched on the triD.

I kept moving the scanner up his body, around his torso.

This guy was in good shape, too good of shape. The basic equipment we had here wasn't going to give me any details but I could fill in the blanks myself. Someone had been doing more than just a little genetic editing. This was full out manipulation, possibly even hybridization.

I hesitated for just a minute before starting the scan on his neck and head.

It would've taken a lot to knock out a man this healthy. I really didn't want to see the permanent damage that might have done it.

But I also really didn't want to hand the scanner over to Denon. He might only be a half-trained medic, but even he would notice something odd in these readings.

The patient's hair was buzzed on the sides, a little long on top, with a few days' worth of scruff. To my relief all of his neural patterns read within normal ranges.

His head fell to the side and I fought back a gasp. A round mark with three prongs extending from the circumference, no bigger than my thumb, reddened the skin on the side of his neck. Carefully, I moved his head the other way, knowing already what I'd find.

No question about it, he'd been wiped.

His eyes flickered behind closed lids and his breathing sped up, just a fraction. Before I could move, a strong hand encircled my arm, just over the cuff.

Steady golden eyes met mine. "Who are you, and what am I doing here?" The low growl of his voice wound around me as surely as his fingers.

"You're on Minor." It probably wouldn't mean anything to him. "I don't know who you pissed off, but it doesn't matter now."

No sign of recognition of the name, no sign of understanding of any kind. On impulse, I smoothed his hair back from his forehead, and his eyes drifted closed.

If he was lucky, he'd dream of freedom, of being anywhere but here. I turned away, back into the nightmare.

Chapter Two: Mack

Nothing existed but fire and pain.

And then she appeared. Tiny, with golden skin and long black hair, and shadows in her eyes, her hands cool and soothing.

The fire reclaimed me, burning her away, leaving me nothing again.

I woke to the sound of her voice, and pushed myself up on one elbow to look around. A long box of a room, locked cabinets on the far side, where she stood, singing quietly to herself as she sorted through containers. A single deskcomm with a cracked screen in the middle of the long wall. Three other beds that looked as hard and narrow as the one I'd been laying on.

One door. No one else in the room.

I must've made a noise moving because she whirled around, braid flying, expression wary.

I didn't move again, just nodded slowly in greeting.

With careful movements, eyes fixed on me, she tapped the panel in the wall and the sink slid out.

I drank the glass of murky water she handed me gratefully.

"Transport can be a little rough," she mentioned but her eyes wouldn't meet mine.

Transport? I didn't remember going on a trip. Darkness, I couldn't remember anything about where I'd been. "Where is this?," I croaked.

She smiled, "I told you before. You're on Minor."

I didn't recall asking before, and Minor sure didn't mean anything to me. She took the glass away and nestled it into a sterilizer for reuse.

"You going to have to give me a little more than that I'm afraid, darlin.'" I quickly stretched muscles in sequence. Other than some residual tightness and an itch on my left arms, everything seemed more or less in place.

She turned back, eyebrow cocked. "I am most certainly not your darlin'." She stressed the word. "But I'll clue you in as to the rest of the set-up, since someone seems to have bumped you on the back of the head."

Her eyes flicked away, just for a moment. And just that fast I knew she was lying. Maybe not about everything, but something.

"Minor is the correctional facility in orbit around Orem-5. Since Orem-5 is one of the stations furthest into the Fringe, they've quit relying on Imperial security."

I shook my head. "This means nothing to me. Sorry." I scratched my again at arm and then stared down at it. "And what the hell is this?"

A broad silver cuff wrapped around my wrist, almost as wide as my hand, a stripe of glowing green on the outer edge.

I glanced over. The woman wore a matching one, but on her it almost covered her forearm. She sighed and rolled over a chair.

"That's your cuff, to make sure you behave. You've been sent here for some infraction of the rules back on the station." She shrugged, warding off my confused protests. "I know you don't remember. The station that we're in orbit around is Orem-5. And people that do bad things on Orem-5 get sent out here to be useful to society, she swept a hand in front of her, like brushing dust away, "until they're not."

"But what does this have to do with that?" I pried at the edge of the metal cuff, twisting and pulling until I received a sharp shock. I glared at her. "You could've warned me."

"You would've done it anyway. Everybody does." She tapped the metal with a fingernail. "Magnetic Access Control devices. We just call them cuffs. Behave, do enough useful activities for the satellite, get points. Do nothing, cause trouble, your points drop fast. You'll know about where you are by this." She raised her arm to display the bar of solid green that ran around the edge metal. "Try to stay in the green."

"What happens if I don't?"

"Lower your points enough, the mealpak dispensers don't work. You'll be shut out of the sleeping quarters. And become fair game for anyone else. There's a lot of people up here for a good reason. If they keep their own points high enough, they don't mind enforcing a little discipline on anybody who slips. Don't let it slide into the yellow."

"What's below yellow?" I asked.

She closed her eyes. "I don't know, but it can't be good."

"Well, then," I swung my legs to the side of the cot and started to push myself up but she held me back with one hand.

"Be damn sure you're ready to stand before you do. There's no way I can get you off the floor if you go down."

An unsettling thought crossed my mind. "This is prison satellite, and we're both prisoners, and there doesn't seem to be much in the way of guards roaming around."

"Self-enforcing rules, remote operation. Theoretically better than a panopticon."

I ignored the extraneous word, focused on my rising anger. "Do you know what I'm here for, what I've done?"

"Prisoner files are sealed from other prisoners. If no one knows details about anyone's past transgressions, maybe people won't make the same mistakes." She grimaced. "I haven't really seen it work out that way."

"I could have been violent, could've been anything and they left you alone with me?" I didn't even know who 'they' were, but they were on my shit list.

She looked amused. "Get too far out of line against another green, and the cuffs take you down. The jolt you got before us just a little love tap, the cuffs connect directly into the nerves of your arm." She stood up, pushed the chair away. "I told Denon I'd stay until you woke, but I'm about ready to call it a night. If you really are ready to go, let's see if we can find you quarters."

As I rose from the cot, my stomach rumbled. "I'd rather you showed me where to get one of those mealpaks you mentioned." I followed her out the door. "Not sure when I ate last."

She nodded and turned down the corridor. "Easy enough. I'm ready to head to the mess myself."

We walked in silence for a minute, and I tried to get my bearings. Why the hell was I on a prison satellite, in orbit around a station I'd never heard of? Actually -

"Hey, Zayda!" A blonde woman passing the other way called out, giving a small wave to my companion. "Running late?"

The woman, Zayda, tilted her head towards me, and the blonde's eyes grew big. "Just showing a new guy around."

The blonde bit her lips, gaze flicking between us until Zayda gave her a smile. "It's all good. I'll catch you later."

Her friend didn't look convinced, but continued on her way.

"Well, that was different," I muttered.

"What do you expect?" Zayda sounded more weary than angry. "She doesn't know you. I don't know you. The unknown is seldom a good thing around here."

"That's easy enough to fix". I stopped and held my hand out. "Hi, Zayda, it's nice to meet you. Thanks for being my tour guide. I'm -"

Only emptiness met me. A flash of pity crossed Zayda's face, but she took my hand anyway. "Must have been some bump on the head."

I pulled back, took the panic that threatened to overtake me and pushed it down, shoved it into a box and locked it.

"How can I not know my name?" I whispered.

"Does it matter?"

My head snapped back up. "Of course it does!"

"Would it change anything?"

I stopped the words that flew to my tongue. She was right. At this moment, whatever had happened to me didn't matter. Figuring out how this place worked, and then getting the hell out took priority. And then… I smoldered.

"Still need something to call you." Her voice summoned me from my thoughts.

I scratched at the edge of the cuff. "What the hell. Let's go with Mac."

"Really?" Her eyes sparkled with humor, and her lips almost turned into a smile. "You're going to name yourself after the cuff?"

"Got anything better?"

"Nope."

"Tell me when you do, and we'll vote on it."

Click here to keep reading Caged.

NEED TO CATCH UP ON THE STAR BREED?

Don't miss a single one!

Given: Star Breed Book One

When a renegade thief and a genetically enhanced mercenary collide, space gets a whole lot hotter!

Thief Kara Shimsi has learned three lessons well - keep her head down, her fingers light, and her tithes to the syndicate paid on time.

But now a failed heist has earned her a death sentence - a one-way ticket to the toxic Waste outside the dome. Her only chance is a deal with the syndicate's most ruthless enforcer, a wolfish mountain of genetically-modified muscle named Davien.

The thought makes her body tingle with dread-or is it heat?

Mercenary Davien has one focus: do whatever is necessary to get the credits to get off this backwater mining colony and back into space. The last thing he wants is a smart-mouthed thief -

even if she does have the clue he needs to hunt down whoever attacked the floating lab he and his created brothers called home.

Caring is a liability. Desire is a commodity. And love could get you killed.

http://myBook.to/StarBreed1

Bonded: Star Breed Book Two

She doesn't need anyone. He's not going to let her go.

Eris Vance, salvager and loner, is happy with her life in the remote fringes of the Empire with just her AI for company. An abandoned ship could be the find of a lifetime, but it's not nearly as empty as she thinks. And the hulking man left behind kindles a heat she's never felt. But will he stay through the coming storm?

Connor is the perfect soldier - He's been made that way. Waking up to the destruction of the world he knew disturbs him almost as much as the gorgeous woman who found him. Her scent, her touch distracts him, and just this once, maybe he doesn't care.

The *Daedelus* is filled with secrets and the results of genetic experiments to breed the perfect soldier... and now that she's awakened him, the mystery of its destruction will hunt them both. Can the growing bond between them survive?

http://myBook.to/StarBreed2

Caged: Star Breed Book Three

No Past. No Trust. No Way Out.

Zayda Caiden relies on no one. An Imperial spy, her mission was betrayed - but she doesn't know the identity of the traitor.

And there's certainly no reason to trust the giant of a man

dumped at the prison clinic, even if he makes her burn with feelings she thought long buried.

Mack has no memory, no real name. Just dreams of fire and pain, and a set of coordinates to a section of unexplored space he refuses to reveal. There's no room in his mission for a woman with secrets of her own, but her scent fills his dreams.

When they have a chance at freedom, can they trust each other enough to escape? Or will their secrets overwhelm their passion?

http://myBook.to/Starbreed3

Freed: Star Breed Book Four

When solitude leads to the brink of madness, only the touch of a sexy, headstrong doctor can pull a dangerous warrior back from the edge...

Dr. Nadira Tannu's work at the small clinic on Orem station was a quiet practice, helping the people of the Fringe. But then she and one of her patients were abducted into a nightmare on a long lost star ship and nothing would ever be the same.

When a rugged survivor rescues them, can she turn his thirst for revenge into a plan for escape? And can she keep her heart safe from the heat in his eyes?

Vengeance against the faceless droids who destroyed his brothers is all that keeps Ronan alive. But he can't resist the pleading look in a pair of wide green eyes staring at him from a cage.

He'll keep her safe. Even if it's from himself.

http://myBook.to/Starbreed4

Craved: Star Breed Book Five

Compassion. Kindness. Caring.

Not really part of my skill set. But for her, I might have to learn.

Geir

I run advance reconnaissance, collecting intel the Pack needs to execute our operations.

In and out, hard and fast.

And I don't need help.

So when a gorgeous woman saves my life, I'm knocked more than a bit off my game.

That's all it is.

Not the shy smile I hunger to coax from her lips, not the sweet body she keeps hidden. Not the mysteries that haunt her eyes.

And certainly not the bewitching scent that stirs me in ways no mission ever has.

I crave her like nothing I've found before.

Even if she might be the enemy, I'll make her mine.

Valrea

He can't save me.

The secrets of the Compound are too tangled. The nightmares in my blood can never be erased.

But his touch sends me reeling, thirsting for what I can't have.

What harm could one night do?

http://myBook.to/Starbreed5

Snared: Star Breed Book Six

When the only woman Xander cared for was ripped from his arms, nothing else mattered.

Now she's back. Fragile and brave, beautiful and brilliant. Someone to protect, someone to fight for.

Except she doesn't remember him at all.

Her curves and captivating scent drive him mad, demanding he cares for her, possess her.

He'll keep his mate safe, even if the Empire burns to ash around them.

Loree Sarratt is tired of everyone treating her like an invalid. Her hacking skills could save the Empire - if she's not arrested first.

First puzzle to solve? An overprotective pillar of muscle who turns her legs to jelly when he's in the same room.

She can't lose focus. But the heat of his gaze sends her pulse racing. His touch steals her breath. Everything tempts her to surrender...

And forget the danger she's in.

http://myBook.to/Starbreed6

PLEASE DON'T FORGET TO LEAVE A REVIEW!

Readers rely on your opinions, and your review can help others decide on what books they read. Make sure your opinion is heard – http://myBook.to/StarBreed2

If you're interested in keeping up with future releases and opportunities for advance review copies, please join the newsletter! http://elinwynbooks.com/newsletter/

ABOUT THE AUTHOR

I love old movies – *To Catch a Thief*, *Notorious*, *All About Eve* — and anything with Katherine Hepburn in it. Clever, elegant people doing clever, elegant things.

I'm a hopeless romantic.

And I love science fiction and the promise of space.

So it makes perfect sense to me to try to merge all of those loves into a new science fiction world, where dashing heroes and lovely ladies have adventures, get into trouble, and find their true love in the stars!

ALSO BY ELIN WYN

The Empire's Fringe – Science Fiction Romance
The Empire's Fringe Bundle
All of the below stories, at a special price!
https://elinwynbooks.com/the-empires-fringe/
Staked
In the slums of space station Cilurnum 8, fiercely independent
Anisha Cheng must decide how far she's willing to trust Kieran
Matthias, the one man who she's ever allowed to break her heart.
If she can't, she risks losing the Sapphire Star, her late father's bar
and the only home she knows, to a crime syndicate in three days.
But as Anisha and Kieran try to work together, the plans of the
syndicate may break them apart forever.
Jewel of Empire
On the spaceliner Dynomius, reformed cat burglar Audrey
Pilgram has three weeks to prove her innocence of a series of
copycat crimes, or all the sins of her past will be laid at her door.
But her quest to uncover the culprit is complicated when she sees
the next target - tall, handsome Phillip Lapsys. Can she stop the
theft of the jewel before he steals her heart?
Raven's Heart
Jayna wasn't looking for trouble. Her plan was to keep her
head down, save her money, and get back into to med school. But
when she overhears the plans for a bio-terrorism attack that
could wipe out the population of her station, her world is turned
upside down. Raven's Heart is a steamy science fiction romance

complete novella with a happy ending, containing nebula hot scenes of passion.

Stolen

An alien artifact. Archaeologist Eliya Cafeal has spent her life in pursuit of this find - and nothing is going to get in her way. Certainly not a rogue and a scoundrel, even if he makes her blood catch fire. Captain Ruvon Taxal likes his life. Few close friends, a spot of petty smuggling or charter trips as needed. No restrictions, and nothing to tie him down. And if his newest passenger, a feisty archaeologist with storm grey eyes, has gotten under his skin, well, he'll learn to live without her when she leaves. But everything is changed when Eliya is stolen.

Claimed

In the remote mountains of a frontier planet, tinkerer and part-time inventor Paige Roth has her hands full protecting her claim against the goons of MagnorCo. With the help of her robots, she's doing pretty well, but the last thing she expects to fall into one of her traps is a handsome stranger trying to hike through the mountains for reasons of his own. He's handsome enough to make her forget where she put her toolkit, but can she trust him?

ALIEN WARRIOR ROMANCE

https://elinwynbooks.com/alien-romance/

Alien Mercenary's Desire: Alien Abduction Romance

Kordiss has spent his life on the fringe, not succumbing to his rages. But when he rescues feisty human Sharla from intergalactic sex traders, his defenses are breached by her trusting smile. And when she's stolen from his arms, nothing will stand in the way of getting her back.

This is a sexy, steamy stand-alone alien abduction short romance with a happy ending.

Bonded to the Alien: Gate Jumpers Saga Part 1

Captain Taryn Nephalia was, honestly, a little bored with her current mapping mission. But a freak accident sent her and her crew crashing towards an unknown planet. Captured by alien snake men, Taryn knows she's on her own to escape, rescue her crew, and get off that rock.

But she's not expecting help from a fellow prisoner - a hunky alpha alien warrior on mission of his own. And now his mission includes her.

Bonded to the Alien is the first in a linked series of steamy science fiction alien romance short stories about Captain Taryn and her crew.

Allied with the Alien: Gate Jumpers Saga Part 2

Stephine Willovitch isn't sure about trusting the Eiztar warriors. She's practical, logical, and not terribly fond of strangers. As far as she remembered, she'd just entered her pod moments ago. Torpor gas had kept her still for the past 36 hours. But apparently Captain Taryn had gotten them all involved with a bunch of rebels, and now they were on the run from some sort of alien snake men. Stephine would follow orders, but she couldn't be ordered to trust the man paired with her - Dojan Cholsad-. Tall, blond, stunningly handsome - and annoyingly friendly - she certainly wasn't going to put up with any of this bonding nonsense. But when Dojan is in danger, her heart isn't listening to her head.

Trapped with the Alien: Gate Jumpers Saga Part 3

Sherre Balinko, the navigator and youngest of Captain Taryn's crew, couldn't be more excited. She might be stranded on a hostile alien planet, but now they were allied with a whole new group of aliens! Her partner in the race to get the antitoxin back to the base is the tall, handsome Zaddik Wangari. But the grand adventure is over When the Tuvarians board the Eiztar mothership and Sherre and Zaddik must battle them alone...

Lost with the Alien: Gate Jumpers Saga Part 4

Jeline Montias, human pilot, isn't thrilled about being paired with Kogav Wangari of Zurole. He's flippant, grumpy and even though he's an engineer and not a pilot, reluctant to let her at the controls. Why should she care that he has eyes like gorgeous amethyst pools and a sweet smile?

They can't seem to stop arguing, even when they're dodging Tuvarian raiders in their mission to get a deadly poison back to the Eitzar lab for analysis. But when they're driven through a set of jump gates to a new sector, they'll have to work together to survive.

Science Fiction Adventure Romance

Join the men of the Garrison as they discover the secrets of Crucible...

Second Chance at the Stars:

As a gifted psychokinetic healer, Adena Thornwood's skills are in constant demand. She's built a solid reputation for her willingness to make sacrifices at any cost. But when she's betrayed by members of her own family, she may finally be broken. Regaining control will be near impossible with her heart in shambles.

Suppressing the rebellion on Crucible should have been just another mission for Commander Nic Vistuv and the men of his garrison unit. But lies and misinformation plague their mission from the beginning. Ghosts from the past haunt them, threatening his life and those of his brothers-in-arms.

The only way out of their predicament may lie in the form of a bribe, but this bribe is different. It's wrapped in the body of a young healer, whom is battle-scarred and broken by a deep betrayal. As secrets unravel and enemies draw nearer, Adena may be the key to understanding the truth of Crucible.

Can a wounded healer and an embittered soldier come to trust each other in time to forge a second chance for both?

http://elinwynbooks.com/my-books/

Copyright © 2017 by Elin Wyn

All rights reserved. This book or any portion thereof may not be reproduced or used in any manner whatsoever without the express written permission of the Author except for the use of brief quotations in a book review.

This book is a work of fiction. Any similarity between the characters and situations within its pages and places or persons, living or dead, is unintentional and co-incidental.

Printed in Great Britain
by Amazon

17751693R00122